MW01714649

The Death Scene Artist

The Death Scene Artist

a novel

Andrew Wilmot

A Buckrider Book

Buckrider Books is an imprint of Wolsak and Wynn Publishers.

Cover and interior design: Michel Vrana
Cover images: iStockphoto
Author photograph: Jaime Patterson from Hidden Exposure Photography
Typeset in Adobe Caslon Pro, Courier Prime, Consul Typewriter
Printed by Ball Media, Brantford, Canada

Canada Council for the Arts Conseil des Arts du Canada
ONTARIO ARTS COUNCIL CONSEIL DES ARTS DE L'ONTARIO an Ontario government agency un organisme du gouvernement de l'Ontario
Canada

The publisher gratefully acknowledges the support of the Canada Council for the Arts, the Ontario Arts Council and the Government of Canada.

Buckrider Books
280 James Street North
Hamilton, ON
Canada L8R 2L3

Library and Archives Canada Cataloguing in Publication

Wilmot, Andrew, author
The death scene artist / Andrew Wilmot.

ISBN 978-1-928088-71-4 (softcover)

I. Title.

PS8645.I4571D43 2018 C813'.6 C2018-903865-9

Scandal turned out to be addictive. Going forward, the movie-star discourse – the many levels of public conversation connected to famous people onscreen – was inextricable from what we all suspected the stars did when the cameras stopped rolling. That became the other movie, the shadow drama: the drinking, fornicating, homicidal ghost in the machine. For some it became the only movie that mattered, precisely because it was the one we weren't supposed to see.

– Ty Burr, *Gods Like Us*

*"I can allow myself to stray dangerously close to the truth,
and all anyone will ever see is metaphors."*

– Amélie Nothomb, *Hygiene and the Assassin*

1. A Single Thread

Posted: 11/08/2013

I never know who to wear. It doesn't matter the situation. When I glance inside my closet it's like nothing fits – like I've amassed an entire wardrobe of impractical uses and pointless endeavours. I often don't know what I was thinking – in what world did I imagine I'd have occasion for an Italian restauranteur with such calloused hands? Or a pale, waiflike artist, a trust-fund baby from SoHo whose fingertips and nails are permanently crusted with oil paint? Or a tall, Black lifestyle and boudoir photographer from just outside of Richmond, Virginia?

Staring at the outfits at my disposal, one hand on the pronounced bone of my hip, my mind stumbles back to the very beginning of this mess. It felt so silly then, to be so ... excited, I guess. Giddy. Ecstatic. Pulsating with energy and uncertainty, but not in a bad way, not with any degree of anxiety.

Which is all the fucking dumber in retrospect. But hindsight's a motherfucker. Almost as much as you were.

Few outfits still remain in my wardrobe, hand-stitched composites hung in protective plastic sheaths like the sort you get from the dry cleaner. I take them out every other day and lay them on the floor of my 350-square-foot one-room cockroach hostel, and gently rub them down with a solution of salt and lime to preserve them, keep them pliant, keep them from smelling of dismemberment. Fix whatever I can – wear and tear, gaps where the threading has come loose. Every now and then I'm forced to dig into the scraps I keep soaking in a Tupperware container in the fridge, fishing out a patch of human skin of as similar a tone and texture as possible, though my options are increasingly limited – it's been some time since I've stocked up on swatches, or for that matter full sleeves, and supplies are running low. The work seems more effort now than it ever used to be. I suppose that's what happens when you get accustomed to doing things not on your fucking own.

Will anyone read this? If I hit *post*, will this leave any trace or imprint upon the world? If I finish this bottle of Xanax, right now, will I slip into a coma and die before finding out? Inquiring minds, and all that shit.

Fuck it, I'm ready. I'm jumping and you're coming with me, even if I have to tie a goddamn rope around your neck. We can hit bottom together, bleed, together, until there's nothing left. Because this isn't just my story to tell, and I'm absolutely, for-fucking-real, not doing this on my own.

Act I

2. The Scorpion and the Frog

Posted: 11/09/2013

COLD OPEN ON BLACK, THE SOUND OF TIRES SCREECHING TO A HALT. THE BRIEF ENSUING SILENCE IS BROKEN BY MUFFLED SCREAMS AND THE DULL THUD OF A FIST PUNCHING THE INSIDE OF A CAR'S TRUNK.

MALORIE (V.O.)
You died the day we met.

CUT TO:

EXT: ABANDONED SHIPPING YARD -- NIGHT

CHARLIE ELLINGTON -- AKA "CHARLIE THE CHIN" -- (45-year-old White male) is pulled forcefully from the trunk of a LATE-MODEL BUICK CENTURY and thrown onto the rain-soaked ground. He lands hard on his hands and knees, WINCES. He looks up at his assailant, a tall, outhouse-wide brick of a human named MICKEY O' (late-40s White male).

MALORIE (V.O.)

I remember it frame for frame.

(Beat)

We had cappuccinos and split a raspberry croissant. You laughed when I smiled and showed two rows of seed-marked teeth. If Chiclets could have freckles, you said. God, it was corny -- but cute, definitely cute. That was one of your gifts, you know; you didn't even have to try -- charm poured out of you like water off a duck's back.

CHARLIE raises his hands up to his face. They're shaking, wet, covered in dirt from where he'd landed on the ground.

CHARLIE

I didn't do it, Mick! I ain't no stoolie, goddamnit! I swear on my grandmother's grave.

MALORIE (V.O.)

God rest her arthritic Irish soul.

CHARLIE starts to weep openly. He drops his face into his filthy hands.

MICKEY steps in front of CHARLIE. He calmly slips a BLACK LEATHER GLOVE over each hand before reaching around to his back and pulling a HANDGUN from his waistband.

From around the corner of a nearby WAREHOUSE, MALORIE MARCELLO (32-year-old White female) watches as MICKEY screws a SUPPRESSOR to the end of his HANDGUN and presses it against the right side of CHARLIE'S head.

MALORIE (V.O.)

Charlie the Chin -- that was what they called you, back when you were still on the up and up, back before it all came crashing down around you like a house of straw. It wasn't your fault -- you didn't know those bills were marked. You weren't no stoolie, you cried again. No double-crosser, no minuteman's wanker. You were a good man. An honest man. A Family *man --* *capital* F, the *Family, the one you don't fuck with.*

MICKEY shakes his head. He moves the HANDGUN down, points it instead at CHARLIE'S knee. He FIRES. CHARLIE SCREAMS and falls over on one side, starts writhing in place. Without saying anything, MICKEY walks around to the other side of CHARLIE and points the HANDGUN at CHARLIE'S left arm. He FIRES again. CHARLIE'S SCREAMS INTENSIFY as he flops around on the ground in pain.

MALORIE (V.O.)

Mickey, that Protestant son of a bitch, dressed up and down from the sales racks of a Big & Tall, he pulled out a .45 and shot you in the knee; blood, bone and muscle turned to confetti, sprayed all over the concrete. He shot you a second time, in the arm -- straight through the bicep.

(Beat)

I saw the pity in Mickey's eyes as he stared down at you, watching as you slowly bled to death from your wounds. I knew it then, sure as I knew anything: he was going to give you one last chance to earn your wings.

MICKEY steps back, moving in front of CHARLIE, and crouches down to face him. He holds the HANDGUN carelessly between his knees.

MICKEY

C'mon, Chin, take the righteous path here. Admit what you did. Accountability -- ever'thing's about accountability.

CHARLIE musters his remaining strength and raises his head. He stares menacingly at MICKEY. Says nothing.

MICKEY stands back up and once more points the HANDGUN at the right side of CHARLIE'S head. He FIRES a final shot and CHARLIE'S body falls limp. BLOOD pools from his mouth.

Out of sight of MICKEY, MALORIE clamps both hands over her mouth and retreats back around the far side of the WAREHOUSE.

MALORIE (V.O.)

Blood flowed out of you like red paint staining your white button-up, caulking the cracks in the pavement with straight lines and ninety-degree turns.

(Beat)

I'd watched your life -- your light -- extinguished in less time than it took to shake someone's hand. It wasn't some stretched out life-before-your-eyes thing you hear people talking about when they drum up the event, making it into something big, into something other than shit. You didn't beg, break or even begin to crack. You took it like the man you were, the man I fell in love with.

(Beat)

It was over before it had even begun, and all I could think about, all I had left, was what it felt like last night when you kissed me.

CUT TO:

INT: MARCELLO MANOR / FOYER (FLASHBACK) -- NIGHT

MALORIE, wearing a midnight blue sequin dress, is standing at the top of the stairs looking down into the foyer as a half-dozen men in black and grey suits file into the dining room.

The last man left in the foyer, CHARLIE, pauses, waiting until the rest of the group has disappeared into the dining room before darting up the stairs, careful not to make a sound.

At the top of the stairs, CHARLIE takes MALORIE by the arm and leads her to the far end of the darkened hallway.

CHARLIE

(Whispers)

You gotta get gone, babe, before this whole thing goes sideways.

MALORIE (V.O.)

Your accent was just a little bit off, slipping between "heritage" and "new world." I smiled nervously, not wanting you to know that I could see, clearly, the cliffs of your ability.

CHARLIE

(Whispers)

Mickey can't know about us. Goddamn neanderthal can't learn we've been together. I don't know what he'll do to either one of us if he finds out.

CHARLIE pulls MALORIE in close and they KISS. It lasts for several seconds and then he pulls away, leaving her alone in the upstairs hallway. He hurries downstairs, to rejoin the others in the dining room.

MALORIE (V.O.)

I didn't listen when you told me to

run. That wasn't my job -- it wasn't what was on the page. I was supposed to stand up straight, back arched, quarter-turn to the camera, waiting for the sky-splitting crack of the first shot. Right then, upon hearing it, a single tear rolled down my face. I waited, hoping that by the time the second and third shots had been fired they would have gotten what they needed and I wouldn't have to live through this again.

CUT TO:

EXT: ABANDONED SHIPPING YARD -- NIGHT

MICKEY reaches out with his foot and NUDGES CHARLIE'S body. He KICKS him in the ribs, once, just to be sure that CHARLIE is dead. His hand is still tightly wrapped around the HANDGUN.

MALORIE (V.O.)

Hold -- one hippopotamus.

3. First Impressions

Posted: 11/10/2013

"Cut. All right, people, let's run it again."

The illusion of our time together was ruptured by a sudden swarm of bodies crowding onto the set, buzzing around one another with practised urgency. I watched in astonishment at how in just minutes they had pulled you off the ground, given you a new shirt, a new suit jacket, reapplied your makeup and tussled your short, dark brown hair just right, just like it was before Dwayne – Mickey – first pulled you from the cramped trunk of the car. They wiped the blood from your cheek, your lips, your Norman Rockwell chin. They straightened you out, gave you some water, made you look all new again. In the rush to reset the stage for the next take, you were, however briefly, the most important person in their world – their bend-over-backward-to-make-him-look-perfect superstar.

I watched as you scrambled out from the cluster of hands picking at you, scuffing your clothes to make it look like you'd actually been in a fight.

"Did you get it?" you asked eagerly. "How'd it look?"

Twenty feet away, standing next to a black folding chair with his name stitched in block letters across the back, the director, a short man with grey sideburns poking out from beneath his signature Yankees baseball cap, was animatedly discussing changing the angle of the shot for the next take with his DP – director of photography.

"How was it?" you asked again, approaching from behind.

The director turned around, stared at you for a second or two longer than he would have if he'd remembered your name. His discomfort was obvious in the vacant way he scratched the three-day growth on his chin, like I'd seen him do – like he always did – when he was trying to think of a way to end a conversation before it had even begun.

"Good," the director said at last. "Real good. Real, real good." It was perfunctory, dismissive, like he was swatting away a fly. "We're going to run it again, though. This time, I need to see more ... *oomph*."

"Oomph?"

That's right, Charlie the Chin. Oomph. Excitement. Passion.

"Feeling," the director said. "Do it ... do it for *love*. You're going down" – he turned his head and pointed – "for her. Remember that."

You glanced over to me and nodded, knowing, right then and there, precisely what it was you had to embody – what you had to *sell* to your audience: actual love, or your closest possible approximation. You turned back around, but the director had walked away and was already deeply engrossed in another much more interesting conversation. I saw it then for the first time: the almost imperceptible twinge of panic brewing behind your eyes, and in the way you nervously rolled your head and loosened up by shaking your hands and arms, ragdolling like you were taking the stage in a first-year acting class. I'd seen others on different sets exhibit such discomfort once or twice before, but never someone with as many credits to their name as you. It was evident from the way you tried to brush off the director's avoidance as nothing special, nothing uniquely targeted: you wanted more than he'd given you – more specifics, more purpose – because you wanted to get it right.

I think it was the length of it – the role – that made you nervous. I didn't realize it at the time, but now, so long after the fact, it couldn't be more obvious. The part amounted to fifteen, maybe sixteen pages, flashbacks included, but it was more than you'd had by this point in your career. Likely more than you'd ever wanted. I'm positive it wasn't you who'd sought out a role of that size, but that it was someone in your camp who had pushed, had really fought for you to take on something new, to step outside your career-long comfort zone and be something more, for a change, than just another corpse. I mean, still eventually a corpse, just not, you know, right away. Someone, perhaps, with a salt-and-pepper perm, bright pink Dolce & Gabbana corset eyeglasses, and who was already reeking of wine by one-thirty in the afternoon.

But you did it. You sucked it up and gave Mister Perennially-Snubbed-for-Best-Director everything you had.

I never told you this when we were together, but I always admired how you never once brought your ego onto the set. You were there to work and that was all there was to it. There were some, yes, who mistook your commitment for hubris or even arrogance, but in time I saw beyond their first impressions of you. There were no grudges in your world, no directors you couldn't stomach. Just total commitment to your craft.

While you busied yourself getting back into the proper headspace, I began to feel it again, a terrible itch on the back of my hand, just beneath the surface. I started to scratch, massaging the skin covering my knuckles, kneading the flesh of the slightly too large body sleeve. It was hot inside the skin, but I tried my best to ignore it, to keep my hands away from my face and the makeup that had been so carefully applied by a timid mouse of a girl wearing a plastic Hello Kitty hair band, which pulled her long, blond hair back and over her ears. When I first saw her I wanted to reach out and pull out the band, to let her hair fall down over her face. There was something there, something held back, held in. I saw it in how she looked at me while she worked, her almond-shaped eyes a focused, steaming mix of longing and bottled ferocity, that she'd wanted to be something more than what she'd amounted to – she was a hopeful, maybe-one-day movie star who'd been reduced to methodically reapplying layers of blush and mascara between takes. Though I couldn't tell you her name or anything about her, I felt right away as if I knew all the parts to her story, because in reality it was no different than yours, mine or any other.

"Don't forget," the director said to you as he took his seat. "You love Malorie. You're ready to die for her."

And you would, again and again, until they got it right.

"I'm ready," you said, energetically snapping your head to one side, then the other – light pops both times. Hands on your thighs, deep breath, you crawled back into the Buick's trunk.

"Places," said the director. "And, *action*!"

And I watched for another three hours and forty-five minutes as you screamed and bled out and died, over and over again.

4. No One Special

Posted: 11/12/2013

The very last thing I expected when flipping channels this past Friday evening was for you to come crashing into my life again. But there you were, on my television screen, all tuxed out and walking a red carpet for a premiere somewhere – North Hollywood, from the looks of it. You appeared sheepish, looking around uncomfortably with your hands stuffed in your pockets, like you desperately wanted to make a run for it as you were sandwiched impossibly between Eden Grant from *Access Hollywood* and multiple-award-nominated filmmaker Andreas Rain. Cameras flashed an electrical storm. I watched as you put a hand up over your eyes, to shield them, while your co-stars filed into the theatre.

"I'm here with Director Andreas Rain at the premiere of his new film, *Child of Honour*," Eden said to the camera, half-shouting above the cries of the gathered crowd. "Andreas, two years ago your film *Only the Dead Know*, both a critical and commercial success, was left out of the running for Best Picture at the Academy Awards – a glaring oversight to many. What do you think your chances are of *Child of Honour* landing a coveted spot on next year's ballot?"

Rain, dressed in his usual combination of dark blue jeans and a black button-up dress shirt, with a salmon-pink scarf tied loose around his neck and oversized egg-shaped sunglasses that covered most of his face, crowded close around Eden's mic, almost pushing her out of frame. "You know," he said, "I don't like to speculate. If my work isn't to the Academy's tastes, I'm not going to try and change their minds. I'm just going to keep doing what I do best. But if you really want to know the film's chances come award season, this guy –" he glanced back then, saw you and pulled you in front of the camera. He threw his arm around your shoulders. *He hugged you.* "This is the man to ask; he's seen it all. D_____ here is one of this industry's unsung heroes. Do you know how many films he's been in? Tell her, D_____."

And like a deer in headlights you just stood there, stunned, not at all sure what to do or say. You just shoved your hands back in your pockets and glanced into the camera for a split second before awkwardly staring down at your shoes. "A few, I guess," you muttered, your shyness palpable.

Rain laughed boisterously. "He's modest. Do you have any idea how much arm-twisting I had to do just to convince him to come out here tonight and celebrate with us?" He laughed again, patted your arm while you grew increasingly uncomfortable. I could see you anxiously doing the math inside your head, estimating just how many eyes were on you at that moment, televised or not. "This guy's a harder worker than anybody I know. He's been in dozens of films. Hundreds. He's ... well, there's no two ways about it: he's the world's greatest living redshirt."

Eden gave her best, punctuated television host chuckle. "What's a redshirt?" she asked.

"For more than twenty years," Rain continued, "D_____ here has been dying like nobody else." He spoke excitedly, like he'd discovered you – like he was somehow responsible for your entire career up to this point. "This guy ..." Then I watched in disbelief as Andreas Rain, a man who'd been called on more than one occasion the affable reinvention of Stanley Kubrick, an *auteur* in the most exhausting sense of the word, swept you into his arms and gave you one of the most emotional bear hugs I've ever seen, arching back, nearly lifting you off the ground. "You did it," he said, practically crying into your shoulder. "You gave my story its *soul*."

Now Eden's no fool. She's been around long enough to know a story when she sees one. She watched as the director named "Oscar's Biggest Threat" in last December's *Empire* magazine lost all composure in the arms of someone who, just moments prior, was an unknown, and stepped up to the plate. "How do you respond to that, D_____? How does it feel to know what an important part you played in bringing *Child of Honour* to life?"

The camera pulled away from Rain, who made a show of things using the tip of his scarf to wipe tears from his eyes, and focused, instead, on you. How did you handle it? True to form: you went a little red in the cheeks, offered a noncommittal shrug and said, "It was just a small role. I really didn't do much – I just showed up on set and did what Mister Rain asked me to do."

"My boy," Rain said, his large hands on your shoulders as if he were gripping the top rung of a ladder, "you did so much more than that. So, so much more." With that he let go of you and headed into the theatre with the rest of the cast and crew, leaving you alone on the red carpet with Eden for your moment of ... glory, I guess?

"I should probably ..." you began, nodding to the theatre's entrance.

Eden, however, continued talking; if she noticed your discomfort, she certainly didn't let it stand in the way of her curiosity. "Wow," she said. "That must feel pretty great, hearing your praises sung with such enthusiasm!"

"Yeah ... I guess."

"He said you've been acting for twenty years. Where have you been hiding all this time? Is this your first major Hollywood production?"

"No, but listen, I really should –"

"I'm not sure I should let you go." She fake-laughed again. "There's so much I want to ask you. Who else have you worked with? What's next for you?"

"I really need to get going." You started walking toward the theatre's entrance. Then, as if to deflect whatever follow-up she might have had, you turned back around and said, "Honestly, I'm no one special."

††

I don't suppose you know what it does to a person to hear those words uttered by someone they once loved. Five times I watched that interview, listening for some sign or tell in your voice – something to indicate you weren't being as serious as deep down I knew you were. But each time I got to the end, the words stung anew: "*I'm no one special.*"

Then forgive me for asking, but what the fuck was I?

For three hours I let it fester, what you'd proclaimed, live on television, to the entire world. I drank and shouted and cried out loud until my upstairs neighbours started pounding on the floor, threatening to call the cops if I didn't cut the noise. But I wasn't listening to them – I was too busy feeling pissed off and hurt and not nearly as important as I'd been trying to convince myself I had been for going on a year now. After everything we'd seen and done together – the lives we'd appropriated, all those bodies left behind, half-buried in the dirt – it was like you were stabbing me in the heart all over again. It's obvious now I was blowing things out of proportion – we're ex, and you're free to feel whatever the fuck you want about who you are and what you've done – but to see you on television, in about as uncomfortable a position as I could ever imagine for you to be in, and to hear you so wilfully tear yourself down, in front of millions, while someone was trying desperately to pull you into the spotlight ...

Yeah. You might say it hit a little close to home. The whole time we were together I lived in your shadow, not the other way around.

It was *your* sandbox, not mine. You made that very clear. And if you were – are nothing, then I ...

That night, clearer heads prevailing, I registered this blog and started stitching the past back together again. It began as a writing exercise: I wanted to see if I could go back to it, to the very beginning and the first time you spoke to me while I sat next to you on top of an audio equipment trunk, and we shared that raspberry croissant you'd snatched from the craft services cart. I wanted to remember what it was I'd been so attracted to in the first place. The more details from that day that I gradually pieced together, the clearer the overall image became. It started to feel like here I was and there you were and nothing at all had changed, like time had stopped for us and you were still pointing and laughing at the seeds stuck between my teeth as I rummaged through some poor production assistant's unguarded purse, searching desperately for dental floss or a toothpick or even a credit card – something, anything I could use to clean up my smile.

"It's okay," you said, beaming, revealing your own set of raspberry-spotted teeth. You closed your mouth, ran your tongue back and forth across your teeth, and smiled again – spotless. I blushed. You rested your hand on my thigh. If we only had a few minutes more, a few seconds even, we might have ... maybe ...

You say you're no one special, but I've done the numbers. Television and film combined, all online aliases accounted for: seven hundred and sixty-three. Seven hundred and sixty-three on-camera deaths in your twenty-one-year career. That averages out to approximately 36.3 deaths a year. Throw in uncredited one-day walk-ons as a background body in the periodic disaster film or zombie apocalypse and that number rises considerably. Andreas Rain was right: you are the greatest living example of cannon fodder to ever grace the screen. And I wonder, and I'm not sure why I never asked this when we were together, but as you stumble ever closer to your forty-sixth birthday I have to know: Why? Why after twenty-one years are you still doing this to yourself? You sink into someone else's shoes, put on a good show, give death everything you've got – and for what?

Whatever. You wanna say you're no one special, that's your prerogative. But I'm not ready to follow you to the gates of obscurity. There's been enough of that already, and as it is I'm running out of time to tell our tale. I never wanted the spotlight for myself, not really, but I wanted ...

I just wanted to stand in enough light that you could see me.

You probably won't read any of this – I doubt you're able to sit in one place long enough to make it to the end of even a review of any of your films – but if by some chance during what I'm sure will be an amazingly meta mid-life crisis you do manage to stumble upon this blog, know this: you're more special than you give yourself credit for.

Also, you're an asshole.

5. Truth in Advertising: Me, Myself and I

Posted: 11/17/2013

My therapist, in all her by-the-hour wisdom, tells me confession is good for the soul, but that it often comes at a price. I wonder, though, if I'll feel any better when all this is over and done, when I've said what I need to say. When I told her I was starting this blog, right away she asked why. "Do you think, by writing down your story, D_____ will come back to you? Do you want him to?" she asked when after a minute I still hadn't answered.

"I don't ... no?" I said.

"Is that a question or a statement?" She rested her narrow Reese Witherspoon–like chin in the palm of her hand while gently, repeatedly tapping the thick black frame of her glasses.

"No, I don't think he'll come back to me. I wouldn't want that even if he did."

"But you'd feel some sense of satisfaction, wouldn't you?"

"What, if he came back to me because I posted our dirty, fleshy laundry for the world to see? No ... why would I get satisfaction from that?"

"All right, validation perhaps?"

"I think I'd be just as angry."

"Why do it then? What do you hope to accomplish?"

Doctor None-of-Your-Business swivelled in her seat, head pointed halfway to the floor. She glared at me expectantly over the tops of her glasses. Crossed and uncrossed her matchstick legs as I stewed over her question. For several minutes I thought about how best to answer, glancing at her out of the corner of my eye as she started impatiently checking her watch, the minutes slowly creeping past the hour as our session crossed over into her three o'clock. She didn't use to do that. In the beginning, back when I first started coming here, when she still wanted to help, we regularly ran over time. "It's all right," she'd say, fifteen, twenty, thirty minutes past the hour. "It's up to me to keep track of these things, not you." Now she watches those final minutes and seconds as if they were the last few on an extended prison sentence.

"Trans ... transparency," I said at last, just as she was preparing to ask me to leave. "Just once I'd like to show myself for who I really am."

"By showing the world who D_____ really is."

"We're part and parcel. You can't have one half of this story without the other." Not if I'm going to tell all the best parts.

††

In my closet hang the skinned and stitched body sleeves of a hundred different women of all shapes, sizes, ages and ethnicities. Each one is a composite, a unique artistic statement carefully pieced together from several worlds' worth of experiences.

I remember in our early days what it was like, hunting for that perfect body, that exquisite, impossible-to-describe-but-you'll-know-it-when-you-see-it skin that would better serve the stories we wanted to tell. It was an art in and of itself, the pursuit – the *creation* of a character of our very own. You were good at it, too. I don't know if you ever realized that about yourself – you were, are, more creative than you ever let yourself believe. I felt in those days, travelling with you throughout Los Angeles, stopping at every late-night diner or coffee shop we came across, watching, listening to the waitresses detailing their life stories to whomever would listen – hoping, praying their customers *were* somebody, or an assistant to somebody, or someone who knew the guy who mowed the front lawn of somebody that just might have the power to change their life – like we were a cross between screenwriters and costume designers, creating new personas as we rifled through the sales racks at the Salvation Army, looking for that one and only dress that some lonely individual had the temerity to throw away. Knowing that someday we'd find use for our discoveries, a reason for why we were drawn to them in the first place, and that they'd, in turn, bring us closer together, to a shared idea made flesh. There were hours spent waiting in the shadows and far corners of parking lots where we could watch, biding our time until a sweet and lovely girl who'd just finished telling us everything there was to know about her exited her place of employment. Together we'd follow the stink of her hopes and dreams to her home or apartment and barge in after her, knocking her to the floor, restraining her with rope or nylon stockings, whatever was readily on hand. You'd go into the kitchen and find us a knife, and pass it to me while I used a black waterproof Sharpie I kept on my person at all times to dot a seam in her skin where I would make the first cut; where I would trace a path; where we would insert our hands, our fingers touching, and pry free her flesh from her bones.

I remember you had your favourites – regardless the demands of a particular scene, preferences are still preferences. You never directly stated one way or another what you were thinking, what you truly, deep in your loins, desired. How you'd imagined it would feel being with *me* but as *her*. I could sense it, though, when we were together, the different ways you'd react from one skin to the next – from the sweet and shy way you squeezed my hand, spun my late-1950s beehive-sporting college coed into your arms, to the way you grinded out so much pent-up sexual aggression with an all-muscle-and-sinew geisha living in the middle of a post-apocalyptic vision of Tokyo one or two hundred years in the future. It was practically animalistic the way our always-changing narrative helped you to lose yourself – your sense of time and place – in whatever house we'd built for ourselves at that particular moment in time.

I wish I could say I'd experienced the same degree of excitement and pleasure as you, and I think at the time, while in the thick of things, I did. But now, when I stop and reflect on our time together, on what it was like being zipped more often than not inside someone else's skin, trapped living someone else's life, breathing, tasting and smelling someone else's air, and not being *allowed* to step away from it, I want only to be able to claw my way free, to step out of all those limp, false exteriors and simply *be*.

When I dream about us now, your hands on my face or your body pressing up against mine, massaging the outer skin of my chest and stomach, pressing the sleeve into my flat shallowness beneath, my heart and body burn. It's like I'm having an allergic reaction and I wake up feeling as if I've walked naked through a valley of poison oak. Sometimes, when that happens, my memory escapes me and I forget for a minute or two where I am – even who I am – and I realize it's because of what we did together.

††

It's difficult picking up the pieces of a life previously abandoned, seeing what fits, what doesn't, like sifting through boxes of old clothes. Adjusting. Moving on. For the first few months after you walked out on me it was like I was running in place. My heart was a freight train of rage and hatred and pain-in-my-ass indigestion, and I was standing still, not working, not talking to anybody. Not doing anything at all but saying to myself – *lying* to myself – that I was healing, and that this was all a part of the process and really fuck all of that, because it's not.

This right here, this blog is my process. So let's get started – let's go right back to the beginning of this mess and do some good old-fashioned investigative healing.

Do you know what I did before I got started in the business? No, of course you don't. You never let me tell you about that part of my life – or, really, any part of my life, now that I sit here and take the time to think about it. "Be with me *now*," you said on our first real date, when I tried to tell you my name. When, that day, working together on *The Scorpion and the Frog*, you had to leave suddenly in the middle of our moment so they could shoot the corpse of Charlie the Chin from another angle, you left the last bite of the croissant on the plate we'd been sharing, turned around and said, coyly, "So you'll remember me." Then you smiled again – spotless, again. Your inflection made it sound so romantic, the words falling out of you like an invitation and certainly not the impenetrable living-room fortress of couch cushions and throw pillows it turned out to be.

Alas – digressions. An obituaries writer. That's what I was before all this, before I got my big break in the industry, before you and I were *us*. Hilarious, right? Whenever you'd read about someone's husband or wife or mother or father or sibling or child and how good and perfect and innocent they were? That was me. It was my job to put a life in black and white and leave the red where it belonged – between the lines and invisible. A person's loved ones, those left behind, fed me whatever information they had about dear sweet [insert name here] and it was my job to craft from that usually messy assortment of notes and half-remembered stories of success a relatively succinct paragraph worthy of sainthood. Because no one's a jerk in their obit – you've noticed that, right? If even a fraction of the goodness and innocence written into each small summary of the dead were true, our world would be a much different place.

"Maurlice Slater [for example], 1960–2012, was a pianist, teacher and inspiration to her community and family in Ladera Heights, just west of Culver City, where she lived for thirty years. She's survived by her husband, Tony, and their children, Franklin and Julia." She was also a serial kleptomaniac and had spent a cumulative three years behind bars, including that time she got caught pocketing the funds from the bake sale at her local Presbyterian church. Not surprisingly, these details never made print.

Then there was the case of Xian Mode, 1976–2011. I remember this one well. "Xian was a pillar of their community who worked hard and fought for equality and the rights of others." That's it. That's all I got from their brother, and he didn't want to elaborate further. Turns out Xian's mother had disavowed their existence (and promptly hung up when I called), and all I managed to scrape together from a solid week of research that I didn't have to do and probably shouldn't have but wanted to anyway was a brief employment record from the cosmetics department at Macy's and a half-finished Facebook profile with a blue silhouette for a profile pic. And that. Was. It. Still, I had to do what I could. Solidarity in parental fuckery and all that. Even if no one did remember them, I had to fake it like they were missed all the same. I had to make you, dear reader, browsing the obits with morbid fascination, checking to see if anyone you know or loved had up and died, believe that this person left behind a crater when all I could find was a footprint.

In the end, everyone wants to be a hero, or a martyr to a cause, or just ... loved, widely and without equal. It was my job to clean up their loose ends and force their lesser devils into memory.

I never imagined myself doing that for a career, though, not long term. I really wanted to write and make movies. True story: there is an oversized plastic bin buried somewhere in my sister's Vancouver condo filled with more than three hundred horror and slasher flicks – triple-A theatrical releases and New French Extremism all the way down to the shittiest bootleg I could find of Ken Russell's 1971 nunsploitation classic, *The Devils*. Think I've even got a copy of *A Serbian Film* in there somewhere. Most of it's trash – but, you know, the good kind of trash. Scattered between art house flicks like *Eraserhead*, *Eyes Without a Face* and everything Guillermo del Toro has put his name to are box sets of every *Nightmare on Elm Street* and *Friday the 13th* film. *Child's Play*, *Candyman*, even that piece of shit *Deadly Friend*. Actually that's not fair. That scene where Kristy Swanson whips a basketball at Anne Ramsey's head and pops it like she's the world's biggest zit stuffed with cow brains bought from a butcher's shop? That's the sort of cheesy, over-the-top '80s gore that I can really get behind. This is what I love about horror – the core of it, the gore, it's real, even if everything surrounding it is bullshit of the highest order. The blood and pain and viscera, it's all grounding; everyone's got a little bit of horror inside that they can tap into. Most of us would just rather pretend it's not there.

Louise said in her last, very short, very curt email to me, dated a couple months ago, that she'd rescued my horror bin from the house after Mom died, before putting the place up for sale. If I wanted it back, she threatened, I just had to come and pick it up. It was the most I'd heard from her in over a year, and still somehow too much.

In some sense, I've always appreciated the cleanliness of death. On film, no matter the cause, once the victim or victims are dead it's finished, immediate. In reality, the act of dying is a slow, sometimes agonizing stutter to the end – a messy trail of unfinished thoughts and fears and failures that gum up the process. Death itself, however, the part that follows the dying, that's nothing more than a period at the close of a sentence – or perhaps in the middle, fracturing the thought midstream, leaving just a little bit of mystery. It's simple. Elegant, when you think about it. All that's left after death is white space on a page. What that space tells the world, how it's filled in, well, that's up to you and what you decided to do with your life.

Death had always hovered around me – a persistent, invisible spectre that from an early age I just could not shake. Dad died of cancer when I was sixteen and Louise had just turned twenty-five. We'd known his end was coming for close to a year, but one year with that man was like ten – which, funny story, was about how old I was the time I entered my room and found him sitting on the edge of my bed, flipping through the notebook of story ideas I kept in my nightstand, behind the back of the drawer where no one would find it unless they were snooping.

He let out small grunts as he read; he wasn't a silent reader. Flipped another page and looked up and said, simply, "What's this?" I tried to answer but stammered instead. It happened every time. I knew that whatever he asked, whatever answer I gave, it wouldn't be enough. Eventually, I managed to reply, "It's a story ... it's mine. I wrote it." He stood up, towering overhead; he seemed so much taller then. He had my notebook tucked under one arm and walked over to me. I moved out of the way and he continued on as if I hadn't been standing right there.

"It's disgusting," he said softly, heading downstairs. "And it's a waste of your time."

"I can do better," I blurted. "I can try."

"Don't," he said, and continued walking away, disappointed. "Why can't you just behave like your sister." It wasn't a question, and I can't imagine he expected me to answer. I never saw that notebook again. In the end I don't know what he expected from me, or wanted me to do with my life. I just know it wasn't that – this.

We'd never really gotten along, Dad and I, but that doesn't mean his death didn't mess with my head. For weeks I couldn't sleep; I just kept repeating our last conversation over and over again, remembering the way his pale, waxy bottom lip quivered when he tried – unsuccessfully – to pronounce the word *disappointment*. The worst part was how much of a defeatist he was over the whole thing – being a doctor, he knew how many people made it out the other side of chemo intact. How few of them went on living "normal" lives, like there'd never been a shadow metastasizing over their entire left hemisphere in the first place. The odds were enough that he felt justified in giving the fuck up. And I remember seeing him then, seeing how frail he'd become, and getting so *furious* that here he was, throwing in the towel, and still I was the disappointment. *I* was the fucking tragedy of this family. The one who hated sports and cars and didn't dress like they were supposed to. That didn't fit the "plan" Dad always talked about – whatever the fuck it was supposed to be.

A few months after Dad died, I got suspended for writing spec obits for the entire senior class – small single-paragraph prognostications: so-and-so was going to get drunk and trash their car at grad; someone else was going to OD behind the bleachers at prom. Motherfucking Chris Taggert, who didn't discover deodorant until he was old enough to grow a beard and spent the better part of five years trying to dunk my head in the toilets of the boys' change room, was going to accidentally cut his dick off in shop class. He wasn't going to die, though, not right away. I was pretty specific about that: he was going to continue to live, dickless and in pain, until his death many years later, penniless and alone. It was after this, and several weeks of quiet opposition and resentment (during which I started going out on longer and longer runs, whatever the weather, and lost weight at a pace that did not go unnoticed), that Mom finally decided to put me in therapy. And I got kicked off the yearbook committee.

Therapy was fine, I guess. Doctor First-Name-Basis was pretty chill about writing me scrips for Diazepam when asked, which I turned around and hawked to kids at school as ecstasy. It was fun, watching eighth graders blow several weeks' worth of allowance on a prescription-grade sedative thinking they were going to get high on E, watching them slur their way through pretend hallucinations, talking about all the wicked cool shit they were seeing. Of course, none of them were seeing a goddamn thing, but fuck it. I needed the money to fund my film obsession, among other things, and they wanted to tell themselves they were anti-establishment rebels who could take on the world.

Mom, though, she wasn't happy with my progress reports. She wanted Doctor First-Name-Basis to fix me up, get me eating properly again, make me right like Louise who wore blazers and slacks to job interviews, and carried a zippered leather folio filled with copies of her CV under her arm everywhere she went. I wasn't exactly relishing the idea of staying home another year with either one of them, so I stocked up on scrips, sold what I could and dropped out of school before the end of the next year, busing my way south across the border. It didn't take me long to find a place to crash on the second floor of a pest-infested low-rise in Culver City, and I immediately started harassing the editor-in-chief of the *Los Angeles Times* – sending out email blasts, showing up unannounced at his office with coffee, gluten-free blueberry muffins and a carefully pieced together portfolio mourning Elgin Park Secondary's entire 1999 graduating class.

"*Fine.* Bloody all right," he said, exhaustedly, three weeks into my campaign and snatched the portfolio from my hands, as well as the slice of German chocolate cake sitting on top.

And I stood there, in his office, watching as he glanced through my portfolio between bites, muttering not-bads and this-has-potentials with his mouth full. He seemed to not want to make eye contact again until he'd finished scraping what he could from his plate.

People tell you a pretty face will open all kinds of doors in this world, but never underestimate the value of slowly crushing some poor overworked shlub's resistance. And there it was: three months after I'd made my escape from home with a forged American passport bought from an artist and Diazepam addict – the older brother of some kid in my year – I was surviving, working the obits section of the *Los Angeles Times* and thinking about that next step: how to cram my foot in Hollywood's door.

6. A War to Remember

Posted: 11/21/2013

EXT: SNOW-COVERED FOREST -- NIGHT

LIEUTENANT JAMES HILDEBRANDT pulls himself from the wreckage of his CURTISS SB2C HELLDIVER, shot down during a reconnaissance mission. His right arm is BROKEN and small dots of BLOOD mark the snow beneath him like a bright red bread-crumb trail.

He crests a small hill, coming to a break in the trees. In the distance, under the light of the full moon, he sees a WARMLY LIT CABIN. A soft plume of smoke rises from the chimney.

QUIET FRENCH WOMAN (V.O.)

It was early April when we met again.
A month had passed since we'd said
our goodbyes to Malorie and Charlie,

and in that time Studio H had been transformed -- buried, as it were, under several hundred pounds of fake snow.

(Beat)

It was 1944 and you were Lieutenant James Hildebrandt. A pilot, shot down on a mission in Northern France. You'd lost so much blood in the crash you could barely stand. How you survived at all was a miracle of modern screenwriting and quick work with an editing suite.

HILDEBRANDT starts down the hill, STUMBLING DRUNKENLY after one or two steps. At the bottom of the hill, only a few yards from the cabin, he FALLS to his knees in the snow.

Movement is seen from inside the cabin -- a shadow walks past the WINDOW and OPENS the front door.

QUIET FRENCH WOMAN (V.O.)

I dropped my knitting and went to the door when I noticed you kneeling half-dead in the snow. You lifted your head, looked up at me as if you were staring into the eyes of an angel.

HILDEBRANT RISES to his feet and STAGGERS FORWARD. Upon reaching the cabin's porch, he FALLS OVER again, drained of all his energy.

The QUIET FRENCH WOMAN crouches down and PULLS

HILDEBRANDT over the cabin's threshold. She lets go of him and quickly closes the cabin door.

CUT TO:

INT: FRENCH WOMAN'S CABIN -- NIGHT

Inside the cabin, the QUIET FRENCH WOMAN PROPS HILDEBRANDT against the ROARING FIREPLACE. He slips in and out of consciousness. She immediately TEARS OFF one sleeve and begins to dress his wounds.

HILDEBRANDT

(Moaning)

M ... Mary ...

QUIET FRENCH WOMAN (V.O.)

You were like an infant, hallucinating, lost somewhere in a dream. My name was not Mary. Mary was someone else, someone far away, in whatever backstory had been written for your five-minute sacrificial lamb. Mine was a shadow part, a throwaway character scripted to help send you off in dramatic fashion.

(Beat)

But I could have been her. I remember thinking that at the time. Together we could have found ourselves a "Mary," skinned her, worn her life or a near-perfect simulacrum of it as if it were our very own. It was dangerous thinking like that -- I envied her and she didn't even exist.

HILDEBRANDT'S eyes FLUTTER and he stares into the face of the QUIET FRENCH WOMAN.

QUIET FRENCH WOMAN (V.O.)

And that's when I saw it -- how much it all meant to you. The way you narrowed your eyes as you looked at me ... You believed in Mary -- beyond the page. I saw it, that ... that spark, or flame, or what have you. The director wasn't in a place to catch all that you were showing me right then -- he was watching you in profile, framing the shot from a low angle. No, that look in your eyes, it was meant for me, because you were Hildebrandt and you believed I was a quiet French woman living alone in a cabin in the woods, away from the war, and you were a wounded American soldier whose last glimmer of hope -- hope that you would see the woman of your dreams one last time -- died as you lay helpless in my arms.

7. If Only for a Moment

Posted: 11/22/2013

Near the end of our scene together, as I delicately removed your burned and tattered jacket, hesitating just long enough for the camera to push in on the previously unseen bottle cap–shaped hole in your side, you let slip one last whisper of pain. You were like a plastic bag squeezed of all air, and in that moment you made a believer out of unnnamed Quiet French Woman, twenty-five, White, with light brown hair.

When the director yelled cut, you sprang to life, leaping up out of my arms and stretching yours to the ceiling before proceeding to hop up and down and pop your neck from side to side, loosening up between takes. You turned and scanned across the set, waiting to see if they needed us to run the scene one more time, and you acted like you didn't recognize me from before. Who knows, maybe you didn't. I was beginning to sense our first encounter had left more of an impression on me than you. It had felt like, as Charlie the Chin, you put the very first cracks in my outer shell. But it was as Lieutenant James Hildebrandt that, in the course of a single afternoon, you successfully managed, with little more than a glance – a perfectly soul-destroying glance – to worm your way into my heart. Being together again only a few weeks after we'd first met on the set of *The Scorpion and the Frog*, this time in a three-walled cabin on the snow-covered floor of a studio lot in the middle of spring, I was struck fearing the worst: I was somehow, unexpectedly, falling for you. Or for the idea of you. The chemical fucking shock of you.

It wasn't rational, I knew that, but love doesn't need to be rational, or even realistic – half of modern music is written to perpetuate this very notion. There's no sense in love, or whatever it is that feels like love that we spend all our waking hours stressing about. As we waited for the next take to begin, makeup artists and crew positioning us for the cameras, spot-checking every detail to leave nothing to chance, I remember feeling strangely angry. Had none of them witnessed what I had just seen? Were they all so completely oblivious to the moment – to the art that had transpired between us only seconds earlier? It was almost impossible to fathom, that the tenderness you'd exhibited with just a flicker of your brown eyes had gone unnoticed by all but me. My frustration subsided, though, as we readied ourselves – you, in my arms, with still a breath or two to give – and I looked down at you and you smiled and said, rather innocently, "Ready to go again?"

††

When I step back from all this and look at what I've written, it's as if I'm peering in on somebody else's life and I'm left with only the painfully obvious: when it comes to you and me, I lost perspective and I lost it quick.

Please, don't mistake this as me admitting I was some warped, star-struck fan or IMDb ambulance chaser, with forensic shots of your bloodied remains adorning the walls of my bedroom – you owe me more than that. What I was experiencing ... it was real and you knew it, too. You didn't hightail it out of my life because I was just another fake or phony looking to ride a barely D-list celebrity's fame into all the In-N-Out burgers and free milkshakes I could put away. No, D_____, when you finally ran away, from us, you did so because I was offering you something you didn't want – maybe something you'd never had before: a reason to stand still. To embrace the spotlight, if only for a moment.

That night, after we'd wrapped on *A War to Remember*, I called Louise and told her about you. She seemed excited for me at first and then she started asking questions: what were you like, how old were you, had you been in anything she might've seen. I didn't know what to say – I'd taken your name from the call sheet, but that was it, that was the extent of the personal details I could offer. When we'd finished shooting for the day I'd gone first to your dressing room, and when you weren't there I'd asked the girls at makeup if they'd seen where you'd disappeared to.

"He's already gone," said the first woman, somewhat bitterly as she tidied up her workstation.

"He's the first in the chair at the end of the day," said the second. She smacked her gum loudly. "He can't get out of here fast enough."

And that's how it was. Once they'd stripped you of your 1940s aesthetic you were up and out the door without a single word of thanks. Whether you'd gone on to another job, or even another city, I really had no idea. While people were busily clearing out of the studio, I asked anyone who'd listen if they knew anything about you, receiving only a "come back when I'm supposed to give a fuck" from the former music video director taking his big gamble on what was either going to be a heartstrings-tugging Oscar-bait masterpiece or a disaster that would no doubt sweep the Razzies.

"So ... you think you're in love with him, but you still don't know anything about him," Louise said once I'd finished telling her what little I could about you. She crunched a carrot stick on the other end of the line, each bite crackling through the earpiece like wet static.

"I know things," I said.

"Like what?"

"Like he's incredibly talented for one."

"Then how come I've never heard of him?"

"Just because he's not a big name or anything doesn't mean he isn't amazing at what he does."

"All right, all right, don't get defensive on me. I'm just concerned you might be moving a little fast here."

"Because I said I'm falling in love?"

"Well ... yeah, sort of exactly that."

"I know what I'm doing, Louise."

She sighed like a bullet into the receiver. "I hope so. This isn't the first time you've uttered the *L*-word to me after a ... was it even a date? It doesn't sound like it was a date, M______. But ... whatever. I just don't like to see you falling for difficult guys over and over again. It isn't healthy."

"It's not like that," I said. "There's a connection between us. I felt it. Really, I did."

"I hope so," she said again. "I really do. For your sake."

"Oh, don't say it like that."

"Like what?"

"Like Mom."

"Fucking *ouch.*"

"It's just ... you do this. A lot. You know you do it, too."

"Not a lot."

"Enough then."

"M______, I just worry. I'm allowed to worry, aren't I?"

Oh, how that grated. Louise had this way of pitching her voice just right so that it cracked on command. It was like weaponized vocal fry. And it made me feel like such a selfish shit, every time. I breathed into the receiver, guilt seated atop my shoulders. "Yes."

"Cool. Now that we've established that I'm allowed to feel feelings –"

"Jesus Christ, Lou ..."

"– I'm going to tell you, in no uncertain terms, that you *are*, in fact, rushing into things, and that it *is* going to get you hurt. Maybe not today, maybe not tomorrow, but –"

"Don't *Casablanca* me, not now."

"I'm not doing this to piss you off, M______, and I know that you know that. Give me at least a little credit here." She paused. "Does he know?" she asked, suddenly sombre.

"Does he know what?"

"What it was like for you growing up. The bodies, the people you ... we ... Does he know?"

And that right there was the million-dollar question. The thing she'd wanted to ask from the very start but didn't know how to phrase. "Yes," I said. "I mean, I think so. Given the time we've spent together, how could he not?"

There was a pause. I could hear her pacing whatever room she was in. "You'd better be sure." She spoke softly, but I could hear it in her voice, that slight twinge of I-believe-you-but-I-don't-know-that-I-should. "There's no going back from this sort of thing. If he ..."

She trailed off, but I knew what it was she wanted to say. I didn't want to tell her to stop caring, or to leave me alone. She was right: I owed her the benefit of the doubt. We'd been through too much together for this to be the moment when shit falls apart; that would happen later. "Louise, it's fine. It's okay. I know what I'm doing."

"I know, it's just –"

"You're worried."

"No, M______. I'm afraid."

8. "Futures Are for the Weak"

Posted: 11/24/2013

"The guy's practically a myth – like, I don't know, Bigfoot or something."

That was Aud – Audrey. She was the hostess at a nightclub near Santa Monica and Wilshire, and one of the first real friends I made in LA, a year or so after I arrived. Aud was another import – half French-Canadian, half Senegalese, black hair tightly braided all the way down to the small of her back. She made a decent enough living compressed, as it were, into a black-and-red strapless polyester-and-spandex halter, threading her Harlot-red and Crest Whitestrips smiles with enough of a behind-the-curtain sneer to announce to newcomers and returning guests alike: "You're in, which means you're somebody." It was an art form, she said to me once. "I've gotta look good enough to fuck, but dangerous enough that they won't think twice about it, ya?"

The rest of the time, when she wasn't playing agent provocateur with anyone – man or woman – who entered the club, Aud was filing a second semi-regular paycheque as an extra. Features, mostly – lots of crowd work filling seats at sporting events, looking longingly into drinks or the eyes of people sitting across from her in bars, or pretending to enjoy a nice meal while the leads in the foreground worked and reworked their lines, making a show of spitting half-chewed hunks of bread and meat into spit buckets positioned just below the table, out of sight of the cameras.

"My mom died last night," she said to me the very first time we went out for drinks following her shift. "Tragic. Poor little bird fell down two flights of stairs and broke every wretched bone in her body. The paramedics found her at the very bottom, tangled into an ampersand." She sniffed an exclamation point, dabbed her wine-red eyes with a tissue.

"Is that true?" I asked.

"The funeral's in three days," she continued, ignoring my question like I was a crumb of dirt she'd flicked out from beneath her half-inch press-on nails. "Naturally, I have to do all the planning myself. Selfish woman didn't even bother to write out a proper will. You'll be there, won't you?"

"Huh?"

"Her funeral. You'll come, right?" She batted her doe eyes.

"Uh, sure," I said, confused and a little baffled at being asked such a thing on a first meeting. "I'll come."

"No, you won't." She sipped from the edge of her wineglass, noisily swishing the liquid between her teeth as if it were mouthwash. "She's fine. As spry as ever, and not looking to give up her grandmother's expensive bone china anytime soon. That sounded authentic though, ya? I'm still working on getting the tears to come on command."

And that was Aud. It was she who first opened me up to this world – told me what I'd always known deep down, that I had an eye for film, and convinced me to enrol in night classes at a local film school, one of those ones you see advertised at bus stops and at video stores, back when video stores still existed. She helped me navigate the unions, smuggled me onto my first-ever set and gave me a taste of what it was all like. That was a long time ago now – nearly half my life. Without her, I don't know if I'd have ever gotten my foot in the door. I'm still not sure if I should love her or hate her for that.

Two or three nights after that conversation with Louise, Aud and I went out for Chinese. Almost right away I started bombarding her with questions about D_____. I was a little hesitant prior to getting there – Aud had had a front-row seat for my last relationship, with a mealy-mouthed production assistant/Venice Beach dude bro named Daryk (yes, spelled like that, fucking LA parents), who stunk of salt water and suntan lotion day and night. She'd spent the better part of the two months he and I had been together telling me what a fool I was, that he was just having fun, that he wasn't really interested in me and sure as shit wasn't going to call me back after the fifteenth message I'd left in the two days since I'd last heard from him, which turned into two weeks, then a month, then she was right and she fucking told me so and why didn't I listen to her in the first place?

But. In the decade-plus we'd known one another, there was one key thing I'd learned about Aud: she knew something about practically everyone in the industry. So yeah, I was going to ask about D_____. I was going to take whatever avenues I could to learn more about him, enigmatic bastard that he was ... is. When I gave her his name, however, it was like watching a loose light bulb flicker for a second, as if trying to turn on, trying to catch a spark.

"Who?" she said between mouthfuls of sweet-and-sour pork.

I repeated the name, doing my best not to shout it over the noise coming from the surrounding tables. She hesitated then started nodding, quickly swallowing her food.

"Okay, yeah, I think I know who that is. I mean we haven't worked together or anything, not directly, but I think I might've seen him around on a couple of shoots. I've definitely heard a few things."

"Yeah?" I said. "What kinds of things?"

"All kinds of things."

"So forthcoming you are."

She gave me the finger. "Anyway, there's not really that much to tell. Way I hear it he sort of flits around doing death scenes and only death scenes. Never really sticks around a place for too long, ya? Keeps mostly to himself – doesn't open his mouth unless you're somebody important, that sort of thing. The guy's practically a myth – like, I don't know, Bigfoot or something. Alex – you know Alex, right? Anyway, Alex told me he worked with him once, 'bout a year ago. He said D_____ was a bit of a prick – went all Daniel Day-Lewis and wouldn't break character for anything, even when someone tried to make conversation with him. Alex said he was, like, the Frank Welker of corpses, or something. Every role he gets he's either a body or will be one soon enough."

"Who's Frank Welker?"

She didn't answer and instead cracked a fortune cookie in half, removing the paper from inside. "Fuck!" She dropped the slip of paper and the two empty pieces of cookie onto her plate and reached across the table, snatching the second fortune cookie right out of my hands. She broke it in half, pulled out the paper strip and cursed again, louder this time. Heads turned in our direction.

"I can't fucking believe it," she said, elongating the *A* in *can't*. When Aud lost her temper she also lost her tight grip on her LA accent. "Five. It's a fucking sign, is what it is."

"Five what?" I asked. In response, she took one of the strips of paper and reached back across the table, depositing it on my plate. I picked up the strip and looked at it – both sides were blank.

"Five times now," she said, "I've gotten snubbed by these fucking Chinese hockey pucks."

"Wow, that's ... that's pretty racist, you know."

"What's racist?"

"What you just said. Calling them Chinese hockey pucks."

"Fuck you, I'll tell you what's racist."

"Also, when you think about it, they're a lot more like eggshells than they are hockey pucks."

Aud picked up one of the broken pieces of cookie, pinched between her thumb and index finger. "You know what these are, ya? They're a tourist trap on home soil. They play up some bullshit cultural mystique, convince us they've got a bead on tomorrow and the day after that and the day after that. But you wanna know the truth?" She slapped the half-a-cookie on her plate, shattering it into several smaller pieces. "It's a mass-produced middle finger for all of us."

"Except you," I said.

"What?"

"It's a middle finger for us, but not you. Otherwise you'd have gotten a fortune in yours."

She stuck out her tongue. "Motherfucker, you didn't have no fortune in yours neither!"

"Whatever. I'm not the one thinking five blank fortunes is a sign the entire Chinese nation is out to get me."

"I don't think anything, M______. I know my shit."

"There's a lot wrong with you. In the head, I mean. More than with most people."

"You love me and you know it."

"Aud. Fucking focus – I asked you a question before. Who's Frank Welker?"

"I don't know," she said, finally paying attention again. "Just some actor who's done a lot of jobs, I think."

That was an understatement. Born March 12, 1946, Franklin W. Welker is one of the world's most prolific voice actors with a career spanning forty years and over seven hundred roles. Even if you didn't know his name before now, odds are you've heard him in something. For fuck's sake, he was the voice of both Doctor Claw on *Inspector Gadget* and Megatron on *Transformers*. So yeah, I can see why Alex made the comparison. You know, apart from all the death and dying.

"Anyway, what's with the sudden curiosity in this guy?" Aud asked.

"It's nothing," I said. "I did a couple scenes with him recently, and ... I don't know ... I thought, maybe, that there was something between us."

Aud sighed, shook her head.

"What? What'd I do?"

Gently, nervously, Aud tugged at the skin of her wrist as if it were loose. "M______, you know I love you, ya?"

"Aud, we've been over this. You know we can't."

"No, no, it's not ... I don't mean that. It's that you have this weird obsession with death and ... I don't understand it."

"I mean, it's my job to be at least a little interested by death."

"I didn't say interested. I said obsessed."

I didn't respond at first, waiting for her to follow her pronouncement with something more – some shred of evidence, perhaps, to back up her claim. Instead, her eyes drifted lazily down. She just stared at her empty plate, seemingly saddened by what she'd just said.

"Look," I said after thirty incredibly uncomfortable seconds, "I didn't know he only did death scenes when I asked what you knew about him. We shared a moment together on set, and I don't think I was alone in thinking that it might have been a little more than just that." I held up one hand as if swearing on an invisible bible. "That's really all there is to it."

But Aud, I realized, had fallen further into thought and lost sight of our conversation.

Though I didn't want to admit it, there was truth to what she'd said, about my unfortunate ... fascination, I guess, with death. Aud was one of the few people to whom I'd told my life story in full – the yearbook incident, Dad dying from cancer and me skipping out on Mom, all of it. Who I knew I was. Inside. I trusted her with that knowledge not because she was fun to be around but because half the time she seemed about as lost in this city as I felt.

It was the fourth or fifth time I'd spent the night at Aud's place after a party, when she was flaked out half-naked on the couch, that I saw the track marks on her arm – a bit of deep purplish-blue in a sea of beautiful dark brown. When I confronted her about it, she cursed at me, threw a lamp at my head and kicked me out of her apartment, only to dial me up the next day feeling hungover and apologetic. She said it wasn't anything to be concerned about – a breath of fresh air, she called it. Just something she needed to make the days seem a little brighter. After that, whenever I tried to talk to her about her heroin use she quickly shut me down, told me she only shot up every once in a while, called it a chickenshit habit and said it was nothing to worry about. I did worry, though, too much and not enough at the same time. I'd grown up within spitting distance of Vancouver's Downtown Eastside, and had seen first-hand what that shit did to a person. One night, feeling especially despondent about her situation, I wrote a draft of her future obit and emailed it to her. Two minutes later she was screaming into my ear, calling me a motherfucker, saying that I had no right to do that to her. I tried to tell her it was for her own good, that I was showing her what her family would have to one day read if she continued doing this to herself. She called and hung up on me seven times that night and then I didn't hear from her again for nearly a month. When at last she came out of hiding, we went out, grabbed a coffee, said our apologies and never spoke another word about it – save for the one time she asked, while drunk, if I'd meant what I had written in her obit, that she was a good person and I was lucky to have known her. That I loved her like a sister. I promised her I had meant every word.

Aud finished her drink, her fingers lingering on the glass, tapping her nails on the rim to fill the silence. "I just don't know what it is," she said, finally. "Why you'd be interested in someone like that and not someone better."

"Someone like you?"

"For example."

"Aud, haven't you heard? It's death I'm obsessed with, not ticking time bombs."

"*Salaud.*" She chewed the word as if gnawing on a piece of steak.

"At any rate," I said, "I doubt I'll ever see him again. I was just thinking out loud." But even speaking the words, I knew I didn't quite believe them. There was this nagging thought, though, in the back of my head, that maybe I should. I was falling for him, yes, but also I was aware, to some extent, how loose and entirely chemical the whole thing was at that point. In those early days he was something of a ghost to me, that much was true. At first I assumed it was performance-based, like he was actively carving an identity out of stone, doing whatever he could to be seen as a serious artist and someone not at all swayed by the limelight. It was commendable; he was bristling with that thing people have when they're not being total assholes: professionalism.

But Aud was right about one thing: tracking him down was initially like hunting Bigfoot.

That night, after Aud and I said our see-you-laters, I went home and jumped on IMDb – where there are no pictures, no biographical information of any kind on D_____ – and started my search. His page – the first of three I found with his last name spelled different enough on each profile to confuse anyone suddenly interested in who he was or what he'd done – was just a list of a few hundred roles with very few proper names attached, mostly basic descriptive identifiers such as "Charred Body in Driver's Seat" and "Plague Victim #312." It was the two roles we'd shared, however, that first clued me in to his somewhat splintered persona: the name he'd used on the call sheet for *A War to Remember* didn't list Charlie the Chin among its credits – they were two separate people. A bit more cross-referencing and some quick math, adding up the various roles across the multiple profiles I'd found, and I began to better understand Alex's Frank Welker comparison.

He's a ronin – a travelling purveyor of death for hire to anyone, seemingly regardless of the quality of the script. (Clearly – have you watched *Piranha Head*? Good. Don't.) I immediately started downloading everything of D_____'s I could get my hands on – educating myself, as it were, on his career and, hopefully, the person behind the name(s) on the call sheet. The more I watched, fascinated by the very idea of a death scene artist, the more his true self was revealed to me layer by bloody layer. He embodied something quintessentially beautiful about film, how flexible it was, how ... transient. Fuck, I promised myself after everything he put me through I'd never use that word again, but it's really all that fits. Slowly, I started to see patterns emerging in his work – waves – where he'd take up a job in one place, sort of settle down for a few weeks, maybe a month, do a few more jobs, some walk-ons if they were available, and then he'd suddenly disappear and pop up again a couple of weeks later on the other side of the country, doing the exact same thing all over again. It was like he was holding his hand to a hot stove for as long as possible before running away and thrusting it into a bucket of ice once the heat – the sitting still in one place – became too much to tolerate.

Yes, I was quickly becoming obsessed. I see that now. I admit it. I could not escape his deaths, so I turned to documenting them instead:

#1: Steven Price, *The Man in the Machine*

Steven Price, son of Jason and Martha Price, passed away late last week at the tender age of eighteen. Young Steven was the victim of a renegade cyborg named Victor One-Oh-Seven. The thirty-five seconds of Steven's glorious eighteen-year existence ended abruptly, as they have for so many children and young men in our unfortunate time of conflict and strife, when the factory-rejected, inhumanly scaled exoskeleton crushed Steven's pitiful body beneath its Volkswagen-sized steel heel. Though Steven's unremarkable life was tragically cut short, he still managed to leave his mark upon this world – a lovely shade of crimson etched forever into the pavement at the corner of Manchester and Sepulveda, five minutes outside of Culver City.

He will be missed.

It's a little rough, I know. It's surprisingly difficult to detail a life from just the character name on a casting sheet and thirty-five seconds of footage – which, in glancing at the trivia on *The Man in the Machine*'s IMDb page, was a marked increase from his character's original allotted screen time of only twenty seconds. Apparently the very first time he died on cue was so transcendent he managed to eke out an extra fifteen seconds of all-eyes-on-him.

I accidentally submitted this obit to my editor at the *Times*. He called me on a Saturday afternoon to see if I was feeling all right, if I needed some time off or maybe someone to talk to. I hadn't realized my mistake until then, and it took five or ten minutes of frantic backpedalling before he relented, leaving me alone with the promise that he'd be there for me, if and when I needed a shoulder. We'd come a long way from me basically breaking his spirit for my benefit. From then on, however, I was more careful with my work.

Every night for weeks I watched another film on D_____'s various lists of credits, and following the end of each one I'd write another obit. The more goodbyes and farewells I was able to conjure from his single-serving turns for the camera, the better the picture of him I received. It was never that clear, more like staring at a person through the narrow slits of half-closed blinds, or the white snake of an unfinished crossword puzzle, but it was more than I'd previously known. Words filled in the blanks and letter by letter he appeared – the bare minimum of him, anyway.

Here's another – it's one of my favourites:

> #312: Commander Epson, *Of Widows and Warriors*
>
> A good man, a family man, Commander Archibald J. Epson of her Majesty's Royal Fleet rose to meet all occasions head-on. One day, he threw himself on a live grenade to protect his fellow officers. That was kind of the end of things for good ol' Archie. Went out with a bang – that's worth something, isn't it?

A full week into my research, I started reaching out. I asked Aud if she could float D_____'s name around a few sets, see if anyone knew anything about him – anything beyond what I'd managed to cull from my limited celluloid-based investigation. Over the next few weeks she helped put me in touch with a couple of makeup artists who'd done some work on him, prettying him up like a corpse, and one DP who remembered shooting D_____ on at least five different occasions and reported that it was like he was a different man each time. Those who remembered him, it seemed – those precious few – declared he was little more than a blip on their radar: he was there and then he wasn't, poof, gone in the blink of an eye as if he was worried he'd be asked to stick around, to do anything more than he'd been contracted for, if he didn't light out of there immediately. There was no personal mailing address on file for him with any studio or casting director that would talk to me; they forwarded all payments to his agent. It was like he was a goddamn genie in a bottle – there when he was needed, gone once he'd completed his task.

My mind wandered to the many possible reasons behind the dramatic peaks and valleys of D_____'s commitment. I watched with rapt attention every frame, every star, every bit player he interacted with while lying on a concrete floor in a Midwestern pub in a pool of his own blood and vomit, or lying face down in some wealthy Floridian's Olympic-sized swimming pool while crime scene investigators pored over the carefully positioned clues detailing his final minutes, and I asked myself if any of them tried to talk to him, tried to get to know him on any level. I wondered, jealously, if he'd found others in whose arms he could so comfortably die.

Aud called him a myth as if it were a bad word, like it took something away from who he really was – something tangible. She was afraid I'd waste my time chasing a phantom that wanted nothing to do with anyone. Another difficult guy, as Louise so ungraciously put it.

That night, our meal finished, Aud and I exited the Chinese restaurant and she immediately lit a cigarette. "I didn't mean to shoot you down like that," she said, noticeably calmer after her first drag. "I just don't want to see you with some undeserving prick."

"We don't know he's a prick," I said, more defensively than I'd intended.

"We know he's a fucking bit player who doesn't like to rub shoulders with the rest of the cattle, ya? Says a lot about a man's character."

"I get it, Aud. I do."

"Ya? So tell me about it."

"You don't want me to fuck up my future."

She exhaled another plume of smoke, and frowned. "Fuck your future," she said, angrily remembering her rant inside the restaurant. "Fuck all futures. Futures are for the weak. For fucking planners and businessmen and suburbanites with platitude-a-day calendars on their desks and pictures of their kids plastered across their fridges. Live right here, right now, in this motherfucking moment. That's what matters. It's *all* that matters." She tossed her half-smoked cigarette to the ground and stepped in for a hug. Her skin smelled like a peach-and-vanilla-scented ashtray. "I just don't want to see you get hurt again. You'll call me if you need to talk, ya?"

"Yeah, I'll call." I gave her a squeeze, and she turned and started walking to her car. I shouted after her, "I love you, you crazy bitch. You know that, right?"

Aud, still walking away from me, raised both middle fingers in the air. "*Va te faire foutre!*" she shouted without turning back around.

††

Two months later, in late June, Aud died of an overdose. I remember getting the three a.m. call from her brother in Montreal. He asked if I'd known she was using and I lied to him without even thinking twice. He was furious. He talked about coming to town and finding whoever it was who sold his sister drugs, but I knew, even in the middle of his shouting, that he wouldn't make the trip. It was all bluster – angry, infuriated vitriol that could not and should not have been contained. I wished I could have felt as much anger and hurt over her death as he did; the luxury of purpose was embedded in his rage. For two days following Aud's death I contemplated sending her family the obit I'd written for her, thinking it might help their grieving to learn just a little of the Aud I had known for ten years and change. Then, thinking better of it, I deleted what I'd written; as painful as it was to admit, she didn't belong to me any longer.

††

In one of my weaker moments near the beginning of my relationship with D_____, as we were busy gleefully stealing the skins of practically everyone we met, regardless of how they fit into our scripts – their fuel for our fire – I thought again about Aud, about finding out where she'd been buried and unearthing her body; taking what was left of her skin and using it for myself, to disappear into something new, something D_____ would never have expected. It hadn't been that long – I didn't know if decomposition would have set in already, or if there was even anything I could do to salvage what remained of her.

In the end, though, I didn't do it. I couldn't. It wouldn't have been right.

Her skin had already been stretched far enough.

#650: Charlie the Chin, *The Scorpion and the Frog*

Charlie fucked the wrong girl. Too bad, so sad, the end.

9. The Buddy Holly Incident

Posted: 12/03/2013

You wore the life of Richard Thorn for our first real date. Richard, the upstanding encyclopedia salesman who wore his dress slacks to Saturday nights at the malt shoppe and his black, nearly knee-high socks to bed, even in the summer. Richard, who made his first dollar painting the white picket fences of his very *Pleasantville*-esque neighbourhood at the age of eight, and from that moment on, believed, in his heart, the virtues of a self-made man. Of a capital-*C* Capitalist. Of the American Dream™ that never truly existed except on paper.

It was late April when we next met, on the set of a mid-century tragedy. I was Eleanor – just Eleanor. She was a simple sleeve I'd pulled from the back of my closet to match the vague, surname-less description provided in the daily call sheet: a slender, barely-old-enough-to-vote White slip wearing a light blue knitted cardigan over a pale pink tailored blouse with a Peter Pan collar. Eleanor had been a good girl – a God-fearing choirgirl, too kind for her own good, too eager to dance with the very first boy to ask for her hand. I remember how sweet and out of place she had seemed when

I met her one evening during my third year living in the city; she seemed so naive, it was like she'd just walked in off a farm. I found her busing tables at a diner in Santa Monica, and smiled when she came up to me and asked with a zero-gravity lilt in her voice if I wanted cream with my coffee. How soft and impossibly blemish free her skin appeared later that night as, crouching in the bushes outside her apartment after walking her home, I sheared her down to the bone with a scalpel I'd stolen from a walk-in clinic: two long slits on either side starting at the shoulders and running all the way down to her toes. I took careful steps to banana-peel her delicate flesh without tearing it at the edges, crying as the overwhelming scent of libraries – of damp, mouldy time- and water-damaged paperback novels – flooded out of her, as I imagined what it would feel like for her skin to fit my body half as well as it did hers. I'd stolen limbs before, a face or two in my youth, pretending I had skills and experience beyond the boundaries of the narrow bubble in which I'd lived, but Eleanor's was the first sleeve I'd stolen in its entirety. I wasn't prepared for it, either, the amount of skin, how little it seems when on our bodies but how much it expands, how much there really is when you lay someone flat and see the full extent of their shell. The plastic container I'd brought for her was too small, and her arms and legs flapped in the wind, caught halfway beneath the lid that no longer fit, as I sprinted away from the scene of the crime, sheltered by the night. I would get her home, though, no matter what. I would keep what remained of her safe and secure until I had occasion to pull her off the rack.

It was Louise who, many years ago, first caught me wearing another's face – a girl in my tenth grade homeroom named Brianna Mears. Brie was athletic and popular and got good grades. She was everything I wasn't but wished I could have been. One day, while Brie was walking home from school, I pulled her into the woods behind her house and told her how pretty she was and how I wanted to be just like her. She laughed and said that was impossible. Then I picked up a stone shaped like an arrowhead and jammed it into the side of her face, carving her skin away from her skull as if etching a bas-relief out of clay. She screamed until she passed out on the forest floor and I continued sawing an outline around the edges of her face. It was rough cutting at first; the stone made a *fwup* sound with every severed muscle, like a steak knife sawing through a tenacious vein of fat. The scent of pumpkin pancakes drenched in cinnamon and maple syrup wafted out from the gap in her flesh. I remember salivating at it – it had been some time since I'd enjoyed such decadence. Hyperosmia, a doctor would later say, one of the ones Mom took me to when my high school weight loss became too great to ignore – an intense acuity for scents, sometimes brought on by sudden or extreme starvation.

When I finished cutting I slipped my fingers beneath her skin and tugged three times before hearing the *schlop* of what sounded like a rubber boot stepping in rainwater-fresh mud. Her face came free in my hands. The next morning, Louise came into my bedroom while I was busy kneading the loose flesh of Brie's face over my own, one layer of skin on top of the other as if it were an ill-fitting Halloween mask. "What are you doing?" she asked while I stood there, shocked by her sudden appearance. "I-it's not what you think," I stammered as I tried to think of a believable excuse for why I was massaging another person's skin into my own, the stain of what little blood remained travelling down the V of my neck. For several seconds Louise stared at my reflection in the mirror, her own face a mixture of confusion and disgust, and then, at last, concern. She nodded once, slowly, and backed out of my room, gently pulling the door until it clicked shut. She wouldn't speak to me again about the matter until a month after Dad's funeral, when she told me she understood if there were certain things I didn't feel like I could talk to her about, that it was okay to be me and that I didn't ever have to wear a second skin around her. "Because we're all we've got," she said as I slowly removed the face and hair of a young woman I'd met only a week before, in a park across the street from my school, and smiled at her, lovingly, as myself.

††

The setting: a town hall dance floor at night. Rather than construct one from scratch, the production team secured use of a high school gymnasium in Silver Lake and crafted a false floor raised just high enough to be awkward. They added some streamers here and there, a couple of balloon archways, a row of punch bowls set atop long cafeteria tables that ran alongside a vomiting of pastel dresses as far as the eye could see. *Voila!* We had ourselves a decent replica of 1950s-whatever, provided your main point of reference was *Back to the Future*.

I saw you before you saw me, standing in the middle of the floor, awaiting your dance partner. "You look familiar," I said, walking right up to you. I took both your hands, placed your right on my hip before you even knew what was happening. We took position, stood at the ready as if in a still life, surrounded by more than thirty other couples, their eyes all locked on their partners as they – as we – waited for our cue.

You blinked then, and I saw shock register in your eyes. It was as if you'd only just noticed the ravishing beehived and red-lipped vixen in front of you.

"I'm sorry," you said, "did you say something?"

"I said you look familiar." I grinned. "These teeth had freckles, once upon a time."

You stared at me carefully, examining my face as you would bacteria under a microscope. Your eyes narrowed then, and I could tell you were busily, nervously sifting through your internal card catalogue of lives, searching for where it was and under what circumstances we'd met.

"Malorie?" you whispered.

I nodded. "Charlie." And you smiled, shyly, appearing dapper as all hell in your pressed off-white slacks and pinstriped suit jacket. You looked at that moment like a little boy who'd gotten into his father's wardrobe and, without permission, decided to try on all his clothes.

"All right, everybody, places," shouted the former coffee runner–turned–assistant director as he swept anxiously through the crowd, quickly checking and rechecking each dance couple's placement.

"You look nervous," you – Richard – said.

I turned to the right and watched as a band set up against a tall false wall to one side of the gymnasium. Stretched across the wall was a large yellow banner that read *HAPPY NEW YEAR 1959.*

"I've never done anything like this," I said.

"What's that?"

"Died."

You let out a small laugh. "There's nothing to it. Forty-five seconds in the hydraulic gimbal will rock the floor and the wall over there comes tumbling down. It'll be a loud bang, lots of chaos. Just remember to go down with it and you'll be fine."

"You make it sound so simple."

"It can be."

I glanced over at the false wall. "It looks heavy. Will it hurt?"

You shook your head. "Not in the least. It's a little like being toppled by a soft foam mattress, only not as fun."

"You've done this before then," I said, already knowing the answer.

"Once or twice. It's kind of like being back in high school: just roll with the punches and you'll be fine; stay standing when you should be on the ground and you'll just stir up trouble."

"Yeah, I kinda remember trouble finding me either way," I muttered, still concerned about the wall scripted to fall on top of us.

"What did you say?"

But before I could respond, the assistant director, whose dreams far outclassed his talent, cued up the band and they began to play. "All right, everybody," he said. "Ready, and action!"

Richard-you took me by the waist then and we began to dance, swaying slowly in each other's arms. You adjusted your grip, brushing my arm in the process. When you did, the skin I was wearing tightened beneath your touch, the sudden heat causing the loose flesh to contract slightly, shrink-wrapping around my limbs, my chest, my face and scalp and even all the way down to the base of my spine.

Then the floor beneath us began to shake. Just forty-five seconds after we started dancing, a series of pistons beneath us and on the other side of the false wall rocked the set, drowning out the music and transforming the ground beneath our feet into an uneven wood-tiled ocean. Couples all around us started screaming, parting, faking confusion and anxiety as our set – our world – continued to shudder and quake.

Your hand never left mine.

"Get ready!" you whispered. Seconds later, a series of even larger vibrations not all that dissimilar from an actual earthquake knocked down the walls of our makeshift town hall, burying you, me and everyone else in a sea of foam and lightweight particleboard.

††

I remained silent and still beneath the remains of the false wall, waiting for some sound or indication they'd finished the take. As I waited, still dressed in the skin of Eleanor, slightly twisted and dishevelled from the fall, my thoughts again turned to my sister.

Louise had been a party girl back in her high school days. After Dad got sick, everyone seemed to conveniently forget about the two times he'd had to bail her out of jail – the first for being caught drinking underage in public, the second less than a year later for being caught drinking underage in public and telling the arresting officer to go fuck himself. Mom had no qualms about glossing over that embarrassing bit of family history – usually trucked out during Christmas dinner with the aunts and uncles – when it came time to point out all the ways Louise had succeeded where I had so gloriously failed, completely disregarding the nine-year age gap between us. Louise had gotten her shit together, made it through business school and gotten a meaningful job as the brand manager for one of those companies trying to market yoga pants as respectable office attire. I, meanwhile, fantasized about writing monster movies and "slash-and-bash porn." That's what Mom called it when she wasn't too busy primping her eyebrows to look like a pair of circumflex accents. "It's childishness," she said when I was ten and told her about the notebook Dad had taken from me, which contained the unfinished first drafts of three short horror films I'd written – incredibly juvenile stuff, all gore and no plot, but mine regardless. "I won't allow you to waste your life on such ... preposterous endeavours."

Years later, after Dad died, following months of Mom's watchful eye scrutinizing my every move, reminding me of all the ways I'd not lived up to her expectations, I'd had just about all I could take from Herr Mutter. It was Louise, though, who, knowing what I wanted to do and sensing that I'd arrived at the end of my rope – and was ready to hang myself with it – drove me to the bus station early one morning. I remember it all so clearly; as I climbed out of her car and into the crisp pre-rain air with my duffle bag full of clothes and a few empty notebooks, she pushed a wad of sweaty American bills into my hand. "Because we're all we've got," she said, "and I don't want you to ever forget it." I stared at the crumpled ball of cash in my hand, understanding what it meant: she was telling me to go, to figure out my life without the spectre of either one of our parents looming overhead. Louise, in her own way, was admitting to me something I'd known all along: I didn't belong. She was the favoured child – the one whose path was clearly marked in front of her. The one Dad had called his special little girl, the first-born, the one happy in her skin who got to take dance classes and go shopping with her friends on weekends. I was the odd one out. The one that came with a list of caveats when introduced to friends and co-workers. The one who wanted to wear the faces of their best friends to school, to selfishly try on each life like they were dresses on a rack – like they were mine to begin with – but was told no, don't do that, that's not what's done. "They won't understand," Louise had said as I tried to leave the house one morning dressed as someone else. She stopped me, quietly pulled me into the downstairs bathroom and shut the door without alerting Mom. She carefully lifted off the face I'd been wearing, wet a hand towel and helped clean my skin of whatever dried blood remained. "They won't know what to do, M______. They won't get it. They won't get you."

As luck would have it, a spectre is exactly what I've become – the gaunt, malignant silhouette of "*no one special.*"

As I lay there in Eleanor's supple skin, pretending to be dead, I managed to play back our limited interactions, recycling the image of your raspberry-flecked smile as if it were a three-second GIF on an endless loop, and I fooled myself into thinking you were truly interested in me, that the kindness you'd shown me in the minutes leading up to our demise was somehow genuine.

An hour after we wrapped for the day, as I was still pulling pieces of foam and sawdust from my beehive, you stepped out of the makeup trailer dressed once more like a human being and not some throwback from a bygone era. Your hair was short, dark brown, messed just enough to be cute without looking coy. I tried not to look nervous as you came straight toward me.

"Hi ..." I said.

"Richard," you said, taking my hand and kissing it. I could still hear your affected 1950s accent – just a little bit more Midwestern than was normal.

"I mean you were Richard, but –"

"Still am," you said. "For tonight, anyway." And you reached out and caressed the side of my face. "Hold ... hold on a second." You hesitated briefly, then, using your thumb, pressed down on my cheek, smoothing out an unwelcome ripple of loose skin, leaving it taut, not unlike a porcelain doll. You even smirked at the change. "There we go. You're even more beautiful now than you were just a moment ago. Tell me, do you have dinner plans this evening?" I shook my head. "Perfect!" and you placed your right fist on your hip, making a loop with your arm.

I hesitated, then threaded my arm through the gap. You were close enough that I could smell your aftershave, and a little of the sawdust that had covered us just a short time earlier. My heart was beating harder and faster than I'd ever thought possible.

"Let's get out of here," you said.

"Okay ... my name is –"

"Eleanor."

"... Okay ... but ... just for tonight?"

You smiled with searing confidence. "We'll see."

10. The Morning After

Posted: 12/10/2013

"I've been reading your blog," my therapist announced at the start of my most recent visit. Absent from her voice was her usual delicately embroidered inquisitiveness, replaced instead by sharp, almost accusatory punctuation. "It's ... interesting. I admit I was a little surprised to see parts of our last conversation so readily discussed. I wrongly expected, when you first told me what you were doing, that our sessions would remain private."

"If I'm going to do this right," I said, "I've got to be willing to put all my knives on the table."

She smiled thinly. "I'd like to investigate that notion, if it's all right with you."

"Shoot."

She cleared her throat. "Ignoring for now your comments relating to my appearance, I would be remiss if I didn't ask how you feel the process of depicting your story in this manner is affecting you."

"I'm not so sure it is," I said after a moment. I leaned back on the couch in her cluttered forest-green office that always smelled of garlic and hummus from the falafel place below and crossed my arms. Outside, I could hear a couple arguing in the street about their order. "Some days are better than others, but nothing's really changed. My situation's the same as it ever was, I'm just whining from on top of a larger soapbox now."

"Do you feel as if detailing your memories in this way is helping you to come to terms with your situation?"

"That's like asking a death-row inmate if a last-minute confession will absolve them of their sins."

Doctor None-of-Your-Business frowned. "Don't you think you're being a tad melodramatic? You're not a prisoner awaiting execution, M_____."

"Aren't I?"

She sighed and quickly jotted something down on the notepad in her lap before looking up at me again. "Last time you were here you said that writing this blog wasn't about receiving validation or satisfaction, but that you hoped to present to the world some degree of transparency – for both D_____ and yourself. Do you feel on any level that you've accomplished or are accomplishing this?"

I sat up straight, swung my legs over the side of the couch and gaped at Doctor None-of-Your-Business. "I don't *feel* like I've even begun," I said. "Every time I sit down to write it's like my fingers start tying themselves into knots and I lose touch with who he was – who I *thought* he was. When I step back and look at what I've written so far it's like I'm staring out at an iced-over lake, and everything interesting, everything I thought was *special* about the other person – about *him* – is muddled and obfuscated, trapped just beneath the surface where I can't reach it. I sprint out onto the ice and start chasing after our memories and all I wind up doing, in the end, is slipping and falling on my ass." I sighed. "In my head I thought I had a painting of a person, but the more layers I peel back the more I see that it was just a sketch."

"That's because you're still afraid," she said.

"Of what?"

"Disappointing him."

"D_____?"

"No, M______, your father. You said so yourself in the entry dated November 17: the last conversation you ever had with him he said he was disappointed in you. So far you've managed to write a great deal about your family life, but, as you say, you've only barely touched upon the other half of this ..." She flipped through her notepad to her notes from our last appointment. "This 'part and parcel' equation. If I were to hazard a guess, I think your father's legacy is keeping you from saying all you want to say, both about yourself and about D_____."

"I don't see what Dad has to do with any of this. In case it wasn't already clear, we weren't really on the best of terms when he died. I didn't even stick around 'til the end of his funeral; meanwhile, Mom invited their entire joint address book as if she were filling seats at a party, and she just vanished into a bottomless pit of well-wishers and future support group professionals. Those people, hangers-on, all of them, they swarmed her like blackflies hovering over a carcass. They consoled her and told her it was okay to fall apart without caring that it would be Louise and I who'd have to pick up the pieces of Mom and Humpty Dumpty her back together again."

"And with yet another striking assortment of mixed metaphors you've once again managed to redirect the conversation from your father to your mother."

I could feel the sides of my face curdling into a sneer. "Because she was a witch. I thought I made that clear."

"But what of your father? What was he?"

For nearly three minutes I didn't respond, listening instead to the commotion below and the traffic out on the street. I allowed my eyes to drift first to the notepad in Doctor None-of-Your-Business's lap, then to her pointed knees and finally to the black-and-grey checkerboard carpet. "You know," I finally said, "Louise had this idea ... more a saying, actually, that if you spend too much time reliving the past you'll wind up destroying your future."

"Okay: How?"

"I'm not sure. By missing out on it, I guess."

Doctor None-of-Your-Business nodded. "There is truth in that, yes. It's certainly an interesting statement coming from someone in the middle of blogging their entire life story. But there's another way of looking at it: revisiting one's history is the path to better understanding one's present."

"Right, okay ... So growing up, my sister had this friend named Peter – Pete."

"Was Pete her boyfriend?"

"He was a boy, and he was her friend, but they weren't messing around with one another if that's what you're wondering. Pete was too much of a fuck-up for Louise to ever take seriously in that way. He was two years younger than her and kind of spastic, like one of those kids who'd eaten a little too much Elmer's Glue in the first grade. But he was a good egg, nice, always had your back. Anyway, Pete had chronic asthma. It was so bad he had to wear one of those silver medical alert bracelets at all times. When Pete turned fifteen, he also started masturbating compulsively. *Rigorously* even – like he was training for the Olympics in jacking off. He'd leave class two or three times an hour to go rub one out in the boy's bathroom. Everyone knew what he was doing even if no one said it to his face. I mean I was only in primary school and I still managed to hear about it. Louise told me that one day he made so many deposits he started hyperventilating and passed out against the wall of one of the bathroom stalls, pants bunched around his ankles. When Pete didn't come back to class that afternoon, his teacher went and found him in the stall. The teacher and a janitor pulled Pete's pants back up and helped him to the nurse's office before calling his parents. Of course, Pete didn't say what he was really doing in there – he claimed he was just having a piss when he got all woozy, and that's the last thing he remembered before waking up on his back on a bed in the nurse's office feeling completely spent. The next week, though, he did it again. This time when he passed out he fell forward and hit his head on the toilet paper dispenser – gave himself a helluva gash on his forehead, right between the eyes. This time they called the paramedics and took him out on a stretcher, in front of everybody. Poor Pete was humiliated. That night he told his parents everything.

"Now Pete's mom, she was devout. The very next day she took him to see her pastor so he could help Pete fight his evil hormonal urges with prayer and rosaries and shit like that – because unbeknownst to poor see-you-in-hell Pete, he was firing loads of concentrated sin into each and every wad of toilet paper he flushed away. Pete's dad, though, he was a man's man, and he was furious. It was bad enough his own son was some weakling who couldn't catch his breath after jogging fifty feet, but for Pete to have actually injured himself while masturbating? That was just too much for Pete Senior to handle. He called his son names. He told his friends at work what a fuck-up Pete was, and they told their kids, and soon everybody at school knew that Pete had managed to hospitalize himself because he'd masturbated so much he put himself in respiratory distress.

"Do you know what Pete's doing with his life today? He's an investment banker, and he's probably worth more than you, me and everyone in that school combined. And do you know how he got there? By cutting ties with everyone he'd ever known – his parents included – like they were nothing but a bunch of worthless skin tags. Now, can you really sit there and tell me he'd be better off today if he sat himself down and took a good long look at his past and all that shit he went through and readdressed it?"

"Maybe not," my therapist said, "but in this example you're looking only at monetary success. You don't know how Pete feels on the inside. It's possible he regrets not taking more of a proactive approach with his parents. He might have a better relationship with them today if he'd done so."

I shook my head. "Pete's dad decided at an early age that his own son was too much of a mess to even bother with. Pete moved on, and he did so on his terms. That's all I'm trying to do, too."

"By doing the exact thing you claim to oppose."

"I'm not ..."

"But you are, M______. You're pouring out your entire life and history for the Internet, and by extension everyone you've ever known, to see because you were hurt, terribly, and continue to be hurt, by someone you love."

"*Loved.* Past tense."

Doctor None-of-Your-Business continued without pause. "You say you don't want to dwell too much on the past, that you want to tell yours and D_____'s story – which itself is in the past – yet so far you've written about yourself, your friend Audrey and your parents, all of whom are deceased, and your sister with whom you are no longer on speaking terms. But still you have not written about him beyond what you've revealed regarding his surface predilections and your small but integral shared interests."

"I'm building a story," I said. "This is called laying the groundwork."

"No, M______, it's called delaying the point. You're being suffocated by the things you refuse to address."

"You want me to admit I have daddy issues. You want me to say that maybe if he'd been more accepting of who I am I wouldn't be so quick to fall for anyone willing to even touch me, and then I wouldn't be in this situation right now."

"Are you talking about D_____ or your father?"

"Huh?"

"I'd like you to acknowledge your father's disappointment in you weighs heavier on your heart than you're willing to admit, and that it's impacting your retelling of your relationship with D_____. So I'll ask you again: What was your father to you?"

"He was a selfish shitting bastard," I said, practically hurling the words. They tasted bitter, like the skin of an underripe orange. "He never hugged me, never laid a hand on me except that time he walked in on me in the bathroom and caught me wearing – He never came within five feet of showing me any kind of emotional support, unless you count telling someone they're wasting their time on art as 'support.' The only thing he ever gave me was this faulty fucking body, rotting from the inside out. It's the last thing I ever wanted from him, and it's going to kill me by degrees. And if he knew that ... if he knew what he'd done ..."

"What?"

"I bet you he'd be thrilled."

"Are you being honest with yourself about that?"

"No," I said, more snidely than I'd intended. "I'm being transparent."

††

Doctor None-of-Your-Business did have a point: until now I've been procrastinating, thinking I've been moving our story forward when really I've been avoiding the topic of you – of who you were beneath all the transient bullshit and the half-minute lives. Because if I'm honest with myself, there are still more questions than there are answers. And if I'm going to be *super* honest with myself, I'm still a little frightened by what some of those answers might be. But fuck it, she's right: there's no one left to disappoint. Legacies can't cast aspersions.

It's the Heisenberg uncertainty principle: the more light I shine on things, the more things scuttle back under the cover of darkness. Aud claimed I was obsessed with death, and maybe she was right. Even if at the time I didn't realize the master class in death and dying I was receiving simply by being in your presence, I was still taken in by the skill and commitment with which you chased the end of one life with the very short screen time of another. There was excitement in the idea that each new role brought with it a new way to live, if only for a few hours or days or even a week at a time.

"Of course it's exciting," Aud said when I called her just a couple of days after we'd died in 1959. "What's not to be excited about? Haven't you ever dreamed of just fucking off to another part of the world where no one knows you? It's like that, but writ large."

"I get that. I mean that's pretty much exactly what I did when I first came here."

"Ya, but you didn't have no choice."

"So you're saying what he's doing is more ... romantic?"

Aud laughed into the phone. "Your word, M______, not mine."

What wasn't clear to me in the beginning, and only became clear once I was too far gone to cut free, was that it was the *only* way you knew how to live, and that with each new role came a ticking clock that upon reaching zero would whisk you away Cinderella-style, leaving nothing behind to fill in the blanks of life number who-the-fuck-knows. And with no pair of throwaway lives was this idea more immediately enticing – and retroactively humbling – than with Richard and Eleanor.

That night, our first together, I asked you over dinner at an Italian restaurant across the street and down the block from the studio lot – *you*-you, not Richard Thorn–you – how you got your start as an actor. At first you said nothing, and simply backstroked an accordion hunk of iceberg lettuce through a sea of Thousand Island dressing until it was heavy and leaden with flavour. I watched, waiting for an answer as you shoved the forkful into your mouth and chewed messily, like a kindergartener, specks of dressing staining the corners of your lips.

"Let me guess," I said, playfully. "Walked off a bus on Hollywood Boulevard with just fifteen bucks to your name and a handful of scattered dreams?"

"You might say that." Your tone was harsh, and you seemed visibly annoyed.

"Does that mean it's true?"

You shrugged. "You can call a duck a horse, if you like."

I cleared my throat. "I –" But before I could finish speaking, you reached across the table and wrapped your hand around my wrist.

"Does it matter?" you asked. Your voice was different, higher, just a tinge nasally. Though I didn't realize it in the moment, I was hearing you – the real you – possibly for the first time.

"I ... I was just going to tell you how I got started in the business," I said.

"I know."

"And ... you don't care?"

You released my hand. Picked up your napkin and dabbed the salad dressing from your lips. "I just want us to enjoy the moment." You leaned forward. "Be with me *now*. Right here, as we both truly want to be. Let's just have a good time, all right?"

"Oh ... okay."

And then you leaned back in your seat and clapped, your demeanour changing on a dime. "Wonderful! Same book, same page. There's nothing to it, Eleanor."

I saw it then, in how you smiled someone else's smile, something no one watching you in a theatre would ever think to notice, if they noticed you at all: you were the sort of man who could be laughing hysterically on the inside while maintaining a perfect poker face to the outside world. I saw it but foolishly I didn't care. I was already yours. When you reached out and took my hand again, creating the silhouette of a dove on the tablecloth between us, I blushed, wondering to myself if anyone was watching – more to the point, if they were watching you, thumbing through their internal entertainment Rolodexes, knowing somehow, somewhere, they'd seen your face before but could not put their finger on where or when.

††

For twelve incredible hours, we were Richard and Eleanor. It wasn't long after we'd left the restaurant that I started to feel inexplicably swept up in it all – in how empowering it was, stepping off the page and out into the real world with you. It felt like everything belonged to us because we were pretending we weren't really anyone at all – whatever we did or didn't do, by the morning it wouldn't matter. We were Bonnie and Clyde, you said to me more than once that night. Just like Warren Beatty and Faye Dunaway, and there was nothing holding us back. "We could take on the world if we wanted." And I believed it when you said it; it was one of only a few moments where I thought, just for a second, that you'd broken character and been with me as D_____ and not as Richard.

There was something to the story of *Bonnie and Clyde* that really resonated with you. I remember that night clearer than most, the two of us on our backs sprawled across a motel bed somewhere on Sunset Boulevard near West Hollywood. It was almost three in the morning and you were smoking a cigarette, and we were talking about our favourite films from the '40s and '50s. As Richard Thorn you seemed forceful and full of a type of confidence that I'd not seen in either Charlie the Chin or James Hildebrandt. It was intoxicating, the way you talked about movies and how you went to a different theatre in every town you travelled to, and that what you loved most was the idea that every new film introduced a different set of lives in a constant state of flux. Warren and Faye were your anti-heroes, in a sense. They embodied for you the excitement lacking in all of our lives – the ability to pick up a gun, get yourself a car and start doing whatever it was you so desired. I didn't have the heart to tell you, 1959's Richard Thorn, as I slowly drifted off to sleep with our legs tangled into a Christmas bow, that *Bonnie and Clyde* came out in 1967.

You anachronistic twat.

††

I woke up the next morning alone in a king-sized bed with the sheets bunched up between my legs and around my waist. When I glanced at my hand, framed by the light streaming in through the second-floor window, I noticed my skin was paler than it had been the night before, dehydrated. The Eleanor sleeve seemed loose around my narrow hips and stomach, where you'd grabbed hold of my skin and tugged, forcefully pulling me on top of your lithe body. The only other pieces of evidence to your existence not currently solidifying in two quarter-shaped spots in the centre of the mattress were the raspberry croissant in a paper bag placed on top of the faux wood-panelled minibar and a folded piece of paper on the pillow next to me:

My dearest Eleanor,

It is with great sadness that we must part ways. The brief time we've shared together has been among the happiest of my life. Perhaps we'll meet again soon in another.

Yours,
Richard Thorn, Esquire

It's a fair assumption to make that most people, upon waking up and finding a note of ... well, gratitude, I suppose, would be the most apropos – most I think would experience an unexpected surge of hurt or inconsolable rage if presented with such a crass affectation. To the point: we'd fucked and you were thanking me for services rendered.

So why wasn't I offended? Because it felt like it was just an extension of the scene we'd played, drawn to its natural conclusion. You were telling me with that letter that Richard Thorn was done – he was a corpse already in the ground, never again to walk amongst the living. Hindsight, however, has altered my perspective on this matter – given it a much-needed adjustment, if you will – and what was at one point endearing is now laced with cold condescension.

You slipped up.

The croissant. It was from another life and another man who was long dead and buried in seventeen different fishbowls decorating the Don of New Jersey's mansion, and I don't know why I'm bothering to tell you this now because you're still not reading these posts. You can't be, oh golden child of Andreas Rain, because you'd never have let me get this far if you were.

††

We didn't see each other for another four weeks. I was on set for a single-day pickup shoot – bystanders in the middle of a riot for some superhero flick. I was skinless, dressed for once in my original wares. The job was simple: ten to twelve hours standing around on a street, waving poorly made placards and screaming nonsensical political slogans at the camera. At one point during a break in the chaos I glanced over and saw you from a distance, exiting Studio C on the far side of the lot. You were dressed in a grey business suit, a cigarette dangling saliva-limp from your bottom lip.

Any other intelligent, semi-rational human being would have stormed over, stood face to face with you, and called you out for being an unfeeling prick. Not me, though. I shrunk down into the chorus of protesters surrounding me and watched as a woman with brick-red hair tied tight into a bun and dressed in similarly redolent attire slunk up next to you and lit your cigarette. Together the pair of you were a time capsule of *American Psycho*–era aesthetics: oil slick temperaments pressed up against the Studio C lot wall as if you were seniors ditching their final exams – because who gives a fuck, right? You smoked together in silence until she dropped her head to your shoulder and I saw you put your arm around her back, gripping her around the other side. The suit you wore was clean – there was no blood, no scuff marks or signs of struggle. Had it already happened? Had you been done away with yet?

You hadn't exaggerated anything in your note: Richard Thorn was indeed dead, replaced by someone pernicious, someone who looked as if they'd have taken great pleasure in telling a class of third graders that Santa died of a congenital heart defect. Feeling uncertain and a little afraid, I waited until red hair and disaffection had walked back inside the studio before making my way through the crowd of rioters and crossing the lot. I aimed straight for you. You looked up as I approached, the cigarette in your hands a mere thimble of what it had once been, a snake of ash hanging off one end.

"Hey," I said.

You glared at me, steel eyes slicing my jugular.

"Eleanor ... remember?" I said when you didn't respond right away. I was suddenly very aware of my appearance; I felt chilled dressed in my original wares, missing that extra layer of warmth provided by each new set of skin. "We were together a short while ago. You ... you left me a note, said you hoped we'd meet again in another life." I smiled against your silence; my cheeks reddened, a mix of anxiety and anticipation. "Well, here we are." I extended my hand, cleared my throat and said, "Rioter Number One Hundred and Twenty-six. And you are?"

You straightened up. Dropped your cigarette to the ground and crushed it beneath the heel of your brown leather loafer. You leaned in and I was suddenly awash in smoke and perfume, sickeningly thick. Hers. Red's.

You – Unknown 1980s Asshole–you – sneered menacingly as you spoke: "I don't know any Eleanor."

"Richard ... I mean –"

"I don't know any Richard, either. Now fuck off and let me get back to work."

11. Donald Davies's Dick

Posted: 12/20/2013

There are a ton of decent-to-good slasher flicks out there if all you're interested in is a double-digit body count and blood painted on the walls. Most entries in a series establish a formula early on, populating the first act of each successive film with a cast of disposable boozing, fornicating twentysomethings acting as teenagers before moving forward and descending upon them all forms of carnage and dismemberment, the methods of which become increasingly absurd the longer in the tooth a series grows.

The best of the best, though, the one by which all others are measured, is John Carpenter's 1978 classic, *Halloween*. Made for a paltry $325,000, it introduced to the world a young, take-no-shit actress named Jamie Lee Curtis. The real star of the show, however, as with every film of this ilk, was the killer – a man named Michael Myers who wore a painted, stark-white Captain Kirk mask as he cut a swath through a small, select group of teenagers in fictional Haddonfield, Illinois.

I was five the first time I saw *Halloween*. Louise and her friend had rented it on a Saturday night during spring break. When she left to go sleep over at her friend's house, I stealthed into her room and stole the VHS cassette from her desk, and smuggled it downstairs where I hid it behind the TV stand. I waited then, until Mom and Dad were asleep, and crept downstairs to watch what I knew was forbidden to me. I kept the volume at a minimum and sat less than a foot away from the screen so as to hear without drawing unwanted attention. It was my first horror experience, and it changed my life forever. I knew, almost immediately, from the way the tension onscreen created in me a flood of emotions – anticipation, excitement at what would happen next – that I'd found my genre. My calling, as it were. Others would gain and lose my affections as time wore on – I had phases for both Freddy and Jason – but it's *Halloween* that has stood the test of time.

Halloween works because it isn't interested in building a teetering stack of bodies but in crafting a believable, often overwhelming sense of dread. Myers is a psychopath, yes, but muted in a sense; no matter how gruesome his misdeeds, he doesn't speak, doesn't quip, doesn't offer any motivation for his vicious actions beyond what snippets of info are provided by Donald Pleasence's Dr. Sam Loomis – that he was, even as a six-year-old child, without reason or any understanding of life and death. When Myers strikes, it's unexpected and without gratuitous buildup; it isn't the exclamation point at the end of a long trail of expletives, but the period you don't expect to appear in the middle of a thought.

He's a man in the mask of another. Who he is beneath that visage is left mostly to conjecture. To this, D_____ and I could both relate.

††

I'd thought the details of that day, when I saw D_____ with *her*, had white-noised a long time ago. I thought I was past being hurt, but I was wrong. Time, apparently, heals only certain wounds; others it tears open and re-salts.

That moment, when Unknown 1980s Asshole told me to fuck off and let him get back to work ... I remember at the time being more stunned than hurt. My immediate thoughts were: *Was this another game? Was he in character?* If that was indeed the case, I was at a clear disadvantage – I had no way of knowing who he was and what he had or had not already been through on set.

But I know now.

Donald Davies, stock trader. Bad deals, worse habits. He died later that afternoon from a cocaine overdose, his eyes rolling back in his head as a thick stream of bloody vomit veined down his left cheek, his neck, all over that expensive-looking I'm-better-than-you suit. Red, Victoria James – real name Leslie Bluth – she was there, too, by his side, bombed out of her mind while he pretended all-too-convincingly to swallow his own tongue.

The two of them went home together that night, after they'd finished filming for the day. Her home, naturally. She'd dressed herself again in the name on her birth certificate and driver's licence; unbeknownst to her, D_____ was still wearing Donald Davies's suit, tie and imaginary expense account. There was no dinner, no dancing; just drinks until three in the morning, then he fucked her in the ass until eight.

She said in the comment she left on my previous blog entry that D_____ was all over her like she was a grade school water fountain. He rode her violently, pulling her shoulders back as if he'd expected some amount of resistance. When she pulled forward, pivoted, tried to run a sweat-and-mattress-fibred hand through his still slicked down head of hair, he smacked it away. When she tried to do it again, he pinned her arms up above her head, pushing them into the headboard, and thrust so hard he bruised her. Inside. She says he looked away as he did it, too. Looked anywhere but in her eyes. When she called him by his first name – his real name, which she'd gotten off the call sheet – he rolled off her, picked his trousers up off the unfortunately rum-and-cum-stained Oriental rug at the foot of her bed, finished her half-empty vodka tonic and ran out of her apartment without saying a word.

My readership is growing. Donald Davies, Richard Thorn, Charlie the fucking Chin – whether he's out there reading these entries or not, others most certainly are, and some have stories of their own they wish to share. As it happens, he's not as invisible as either one of us might have thought.

It's only fair this time we both be sheared to the bone.

12. Apocalypse Tomorrow

Posted: 01/07/2014

When I first started down this road two months ago, blogging my life story, I didn't think it would be like this – I never imagined how exhausting it would be to put it all out there, to document every small, shitty moment on the path to enlightenment. No, *enlightenment*'s the wrong word. Acceptance. That's what they call it in AA, right? You accept the path you've walked and every door closed off or kicked down along the way. You admit you're powerless to do anything to change what's already been done. It's like when you start pulling off a bandage but you're going too slow and it's plucking out the hairs from your arm one by one, but you can't stop, you can't put it back on again because it won't stick the same – you've already broken the seal between the adhesive and your skin. All you can do is keep pulling, a hair at a time, until you're ready for that final tug. It will hurt – you know it will hurt – but you aren't ready to get it over with, not just yet, because the moment-to-moment suffering is all a part of the healing process. It helps reveal, a little bit at a time, the shadows looking back over their shoulders at you, questioning how it was you got yourself in this situation in the first place. Those hairs you've been pulling out, they're micro-judgments, hesitant shreds of trauma, fear and doubt.

It was early June, if I'm remembering the timeline correctly, just a couple of weeks since Donald Davies–you not-so-discretely told me to fuck off. We were together again on the set of a post-apocalyptic human drama: I was Claudette Winters, you were Garrett Winters, my brother-from-a-fictional-mother, older by a year and wiser by five – thank you, totally not-sexist liner notes. The role was more than just another walk-on; we were part of a convoy of refugees fleeing a disaster of Roland Emmerich proportions: forests aflame, volcanoes erupting on every continent, water levels rising, et cetera. Our basic survival was boxed in by a cathedral of green screens and off-set guidance – a constant string of reminders dictating the nature of the terror bearing down on us and from which direction(s) it came. Behind the scenes we called ourselves the Pity Party because every one of us – save our fearless, square-jawed, face-on-the-poster leader – was going to die, and die horribly. It was, for most of us soon-to-be-departed, a few days' work – a week for you and me, the lucky final pair of hangers-on.

I'm not afraid to reveal, here and now, how on edge I felt being with you again. No, not on edge, that's not right. Scared. Actually sort of terrified because I didn't have the faintest idea what to expect. It wasn't until recently I learned, via comments and private emails from your red-headed former co-star, the squalid details of your time as Donald Davies. So yeah, when I saw you that day, for the first time in weeks, I was less than comfortable in your presence. Confusingly enough, you seemed fine – better than fine, you were acting ... well, "normal" might be a stretch, but it's the tightest shoe, Cinderella.

Our first day together you came up to me and wrapped me in your arms as if you'd been waiting days for me to return to you.

"Claudette," you said warmly, in yet another voice, one I didn't recognize. You pulled away then, sensing my hesitation. "What's wrong?"

"You don't ... do you remember me?" I asked, honestly not sure how you'd respond.

You smirked. "Of course I remember you. Don't be an idiot."

But who? I thought to myself, *Who was it you remembered? Were you in character, speaking to your scripted sister? Or did you for a brief moment remember the bed you'd shared with Eleanor? Or were you, by some miracle, talking to the real me whose name you still hadn't bothered to learn?*

The director walked right between us then, shouting, "All right, everybody, let's get this show on the road."

You turned to me as Garrett and said, "Are you ready?"

It was with such tenderness, too, like how one might speak to their actual sibling or family member – tender, but altogether unearned. "I don't know," I said. "I've not had a whole lot of experience."

"There's nothing to it. Keep track of your lines and the timing, and you'll be fine. It's like being back in high school."

"Just roll with the punches," I said.

You showed me every white lie in your mouth. "Exactly."

††

Filming was a disaster. I kept fucking up this one line: I was supposed to say to our hero, "You don't know what the fuck you're doing, do you?" but I kept going, "Do you know what the fuck you're doing?" or "Did you fucking mean to do that?" In fact, I flubbed my dialogue so much our strong-willed movie star on his fresh from the D-list exile started accusing me of trying to derail his chance at redemption. He was afraid his Travolta-esque rise from mid-career obscurity was being jeopardized by some two-bit extra who couldn't keep their eyes off the nobody with the Dick Tracy chin. By the fourth or fifth time I'd fucked up and failed to ask our dauntless leader what hope there was to be found in such dire circumstances, I began to feel my less-than-substantial paycheque fading into the darkness.

I should have had my mind on the job. Not on you and the game you were so obviously ... No, fuck it, I can't do this anymore.

It wasn't a game and I knew that – I know that, and I'm not sure why I'm affording your actions even that much justification.

"What's going on?" you whispered to me, as D_____ and *not* as Garrett, when we cut for the umpteenth time. "If you're not careful you're going to get canned."

"What do you care?" I snapped. I went to turn away and you grabbed my upper arm, spinning me back around to face you. I yanked free. "*Don't* do that again."

"I don't get it – have I done something to you?" you asked, genuinely flabbergasted.

Yes, you said those exact. Fucking. Words. "Have you done something to me? Are you serious right now?"

"If I don't look it, I'll try a little harder." You playfully furrowed your brow – the absolute wrong fucking timing for cute.

"How about telling me to fuck off? That ring any bells for you?"

"I don't know what you're –"

"Fine. How about sleeping with me and sticking me with a 'Farewell cruel world' goodbye letter?" My skin was on fire; I felt blistering heat blossoming just beneath Claudette's ivory skin.

"Now wait just a moment –"

"No, fuck you, Richard, or Garrett, or whoever it is you want to be for the rest of this shoot. Find someone else's head to screw with." And I walked past you, leaving you slack-jawed and trailing behind. "Now hurry up and let's go be brother and sister."

††

Upon picking up my jacket at the end of the day I found a folded-over triangle of white paper poking out from one of the pockets. It was a note: *Meet me at the Galaxy after midnight.* You'd signed it, too – with just an initial, but it was yours, the genuine article, and it was more than I'd gotten so far.

I still have that note, you know. Sometimes I take it out and look at it, and I wonder what it must be like to be you and to be so unfairly forced into passport offices and filing your taxes like everyone else – to have to sign your identity to anything at all. It's why you've never owned a car, right? Or for that matter a house, a credit card or even a mobile phone? For some people the idea of a social security number is cause enough for hyperbole – *the government's watching my every move, none of us are safe*, all that pomp and lunacy. For you, though, it seemed personal. I'm almost embarrassed at how long it took me to see the obvious staring me right in the eyes: you're happier skirting the belt of awareness because you don't really want to be anybody at all, and this way you don't have to.

I'd only been to the Galaxy Drive-In in Santa Barbara once, several years back with Aud and some of her friends for a triple-header of *The Evil Dead*, *Evil Dead 2* and *Army of Darkness*. I remember the five of us crammed into a rusted autumn-orange Dodge Charger, smoking shitty skunkweed while the leather seats scratched white tennis racquets into my thighs. Aud loudly parroted every single one of Bruce Campbell's one-liners like they were her own. I don't think any of us were really paying attention to the films, but it didn't matter.

I arrived the night of our encounter a few minutes before midnight. I was wearing a dark hoodie that hid my irritated true skin beneath the heavy fabric. The Galaxy was in ruins. It had shut down about a year and a half earlier; the entrance was blocked with a thick knot of chain, a DO NOT ENTER sign hanging from the centre. The lot itself was a debris field of beer cans, broken bottles, empty potato chip bags and discarded popcorn containers. The air was ash and gasoline, so thick you could almost taste it. All that remained of the actual drive-in was a large screen at the far end of the field that had been slashed and carved into a Swiss cheese shadow of its former glory. All was quiet, save the sounds of distant traffic. I ducked under the useless barricade and walked into the middle of the field. The entire time I was thinking that I should have told someone where I was going – I should have called Aud, begged her to come along and hide somewhere off to the side, to stick to the darkness unless I needed protection.

"I wasn't sure you'd come."

I spun, momentarily frenzied, trying to pinpoint from which direction your voice was coming – or which version of you I was even there to meet.

"I wasn't sure *you'd* show," I shot back at the dark.

"I set this up, didn't I?"

"Yeah, but which one of you?"

There was silence. I'd struck a nerve.

"I used to come here all the time," you said, sidestepping my prod. "When I was little. Every few weeks Mom would pick me up from school and we'd play hooky for the rest of the day, to give Dad some rest. He drove a truck cross-country for a soda company, and when he came home after being on the road ... she said he needed time to himself, to sleep, so we'd come here and have ourselves a marathon, stay way past my bedtime; we'd see whatever they had on hand, sometimes more than once. Back in the day, this place was something else. They used to do these themed weekends where they'd celebrate a director's new film by showing highlights from their back catalogue. It was a family place back then – not at all like what it became."

"You talk about this place like it had a pulse." I heard footsteps slowly circling, gravel crunching underfoot, though their source remained invisible.

"Didn't it?"

"It was a drive-in."

"It was a cultural pocket – this little piece of land, out here in the middle of nowhere, was a film nerd tent revival. Haven't you ever thought about the greatness that a drive-in represents?"

"No, I really can't say that I have." I was getting frustrated. You were clearly attempting to spin a yarn for me but I'd long since lost the plot. "D_____, why did you bring me out here?"

"I practically lived for this place when I was a kid." You spoke as if I'd said nothing at all. "It was exciting, just getting lost in the dark for a couple of hours. Knowing that when the last reel finished and the screen went white, you'd find your way home again."

"You know my name. I know you do."

"Back then I didn't know a single thing about making movies. I just knew I wanted to be a part of it all, somehow. It felt right, you know? Like destiny."

"My real name. I want to hear you say it."

"No," you said suddenly.

"No?"

"No."

"Why the hell not?"

"Because it's not important. No one comes to this town to talk about their past – about who they were or the things they left behind. Names and faces, they don't really matter here. It's the story you want to tell, that's what counts; not who starred in what or who's making twenty million a picture. Movie stars these days are nothing without their names to protect them, whether they use their real names or not." You fell silent for several seconds. I listened again for the sound of your feet, crunching gravel or trash or accidentally kicking a bottle – anything that might help pinpoint your location. "This place used to be a temple," you said, sounding defeated. "Now look at it – there's nothing left but a slashed up tombstone and a field of broken bones."

"If you hate it all so much –"

"But I don't. I love it and miss what it once was. That feeling you got before you became aware of it all, of the artifice of this whole thing – when you could sit in the dark with a hundred people, and you didn't know them and they didn't know you but you were all there together, experiencing the very same fiction ... it was like nothing else. Now it's so-and-so's movie, and we care more about what it cost to make and what kind of box office it brings in than what the film is actually trying to say. Without realizing it, we've allowed ourselves to be saddled with extraneous stories, shadow stories we don't need or want to know, and they distract us from the things we should actually be caring about. I subscribe to what this industry used to be, and to the kind of storytelling you and I embody."

"Oh, yeah? And what's that?" I asked.

More silence. A hand cut through the dark, gripped my shoulder from behind. I jumped, nearly pissed myself. It hurt – my skin beneath the hoodie was tender, red and inflamed. I'd sweated inside the sleeve I'd worn earlier that day, and some of the solution used to treat it had seeped into my pores.

"Don't turn around," you said to my left ear.

"What is it we embody?" I asked again. "What am I to you?"

"We're one and the same, you and I." Your tone had grown mysterious, almost ominous. "We're transient. I saw it in you the very first time we spoke, how easily you slipped into something new ... Your desire to shed your skin, it's the same as mine."

"It's not," I said. "It's ... it's just work."

"No, it's more than that. You and I are here to live a thousand lives and vanish just as easily as we first appeared. What we do, it's the single greatest freedom in the world – *if* you embrace it. That's what we embody, that's what we bring to the table: storytelling at its most pure." Your grip slackened then and I felt you pull away. There was an immediate wave of relief as your hand left my shoulder. I reached up to massage the now-aching spot. When I turned around to look for you, you'd vanished and I was left alone in the Galaxy's void.

13. From One Transient to Another

Posted: 01/12/2014

I've thought a lot in the weeks and months since that night at the Galaxy, about the lie you so expertly sold me. That bit about freedom – to be who we wanted to be, live how we wanted to live – it was absolutely true, but the subtext with which you laced it was like arsenic at the bottom of a drinking glass. Louise saw it long before I did. She tried to warn me, but I was (unfortunately, expectedly) too stubborn to listen.

I've thought a lot about that word, too: *transient*. You made it sound like something glamorous, whispering it over my shoulder like you wanted to ask me to prom but were too shy to do it to my face. But *transient* isn't anything glamorous or romantic. It isn't even all that nice. Do you know its synonyms? *Ephemeral*, *fleeting*, *passing*, *short-lived*, *volatile* – actually I kind of like that one. *Insubstantial*. *Temporal*.

Temporary.

††

Recently, I've found myself thinking a great deal about the future and all the things I want to do or try while I still have the time. Invariably, I come back to something I used to wonder about when I was younger: what it would be like to have a career as a foley artist. It was something that crossed my mind every now and then, when I was still living at home and the writing wasn't going as well as I'd have liked. When you break it down, the work of a foley artist is piecemeal, invisible. For them, to succeed is to craft the closest approximation to the sounds we perceive – or *think* we perceive – as natural, so that no sore thumbs exist, no hollow footfalls on solid concrete or tears in the fabric of reality, like when you see someone onscreen using a computer but you can tell that the audio's been lifted straight from the soundboard of a 1981 *Galaga* arcade cabinet. Do you know, for example, what it is that gives a lightsaber its telltale hum? Idling motors from old movie projectors and the interference from a television or microphone. Just fucking *wild.*

When I think now about what it is a foley artist does and how they do it, dissecting the world through soundscapes, I wonder what they might lack to better foster their preternatural awareness of sounds and noise. Because it's a trade-off, right? That's how gifts work – you get something extra in exchange for something else. I imagine most of them are half-blind, or can't taste or smell for shit; I picture them as athletes with left legs three inches shorter than their rights, forever hobbling, compensating. Me? I smell everything. It's the hyperosmia – it's never really gone away, regardless of the way my weight's fluctuated over the years, and it only increases the further I drop to better fit each new skin. That's my gift, or curse, I guess. This world is thick with layers of scent, each a memory of its own. We wear smells like points on a map showing where we've been, what we've done, what we love or eat or even our addictions and failings. We reek equally of failure and success. Smells are earthy. Real. Sounds ... sounds can be faked. They can be falsehoods. Lies. A scent or stench, however, can only be masked so much, and will hurl you back in time like nothing else.

What sound does a gun make when it's fired? Does it change when fired at a person instead of a lifeless target? How about the sick slide of a butcher's blade slipping between someone's ribs, puncturing tissue, lung ...

This is the world you live in – the promotion of death via makeup and guns that fire blanks. The more I think about it, the more I revisit our conversation at the Galaxy Drive-In, the less sense it all makes: each life on film, no matter how short, no matter how quickly death's approach, is immortalized. It's the nature of the beast that the work you do in this industry will outlive you. The better the job you do, the greater the likelihood of gaining recognition for your hard work – and no one, my dear D_____, works harder than you. I watched so many times as you sank, completely, into a nothing role, into a twenty-second spin as a faceless soldier running into a battle you were destined to lose. What if what you wanted more than anything was to disappear and forget all the lives you've led? Why would you do something that seems, at least on the surface, so at odds with the life you wish you'd had?

Doctor None-of-Your-Business called it months ago, when I first started talking about you and I and us. She was quick to say that you probably have no idea what you really want out of life, that you've likely never had a plan and move from role to role without ever looking into a mirror because you're always searching for something to help you better define yourself. Only you never find it and you never will because we both know it goes a lot deeper than that. Maybe you should speak to someone about this, really get to the bottom of your shit. I know a person. She'd probably love to hear the other side of this mess.

††

It was late June, and our last day together as brother and sister. We died in each other's arms as our hero desperately tried to save what remained of our radiation-poisoned convoy. Stragglers picked up along our journey would survive to rebuild, to start a new society from the ashes of the old and to lay the groundwork for the sequel due out by next Christmas. They buried us in a field, where the cold winter ground had not yet frozen. Heads were hung and prayers uttered, carried on the wind with what I imagined would be a sweeping orchestral score. I watched from afar as our former companions cried spritzed tears over our empty graves.

I searched for you in the aftermath, but you'd already gone.

My expectations had gotten the better of me yet again. Following our meeting at the Galaxy you'd acted different. Cordial. For the rest of the week you helped me prepare our lines; you brought me coffee and snacks from craft services; you even helped me adjust Claudette's sleeve, massaging its features so that her skin was indistinguishable from my own. "There we go," you said, once more pressing your thumb to my cheek just below the eye, smoothing out my skin exactly as you'd done with Eleanor. We hadn't seen each other at all outside of work, but I thought ... once the job was done we might have taken some time, talked a bit about what was next. For us I mean – assuming, foolishly as I was, that there was even an "us" to talk about. However, it seemed you had better things to do than stick around for your funeral.

That night I learned about Aud. On the phone, her brother could barely contain his rage, tripping between English and Quebecois French when he lost control and started shouting into the receiver. He wanted to know if I knew which of her friends might have sold her the stuff that killed her. I didn't – for better or worse, Aud had kept me out of all that. But that did nothing to satisfy his hurt; he called me a worthless piece of shit, said me and every single one of her rotten LA friends were to blame for what happened to his sister. I didn't try to fight him; this wasn't about getting the facts right and figuring out what had gone wrong or who was to blame. It was about grieving. He wasn't ready yet to accept Aud's agency in what had happened. That would mean addressing his own neglect in missing or ignoring whatever warning signs there might have been, given his sister's penchant for self-destruction, which, far as I knew, went back many years before we'd ever met.

"Live hard and leave a beautiful corpse," she'd shouted to me over drinks at a club, and then more drinks, to celebrate my first gig as an extra. "That's what Jack Dean said, right?"

"It's James Dean, and I'm fairly sure no one has ever actually said –"

She punched me hard in the bicep. "Jee-zus! Lighten up, ya? It's Hollywood! This fucking town is ours!"

That was Aud, really and truly. It's how she'd want me to remember her – a gasoline-soaked rag tossed over the spark of this brilliant, hideous town.

I called Louise that same night. I didn't tell her about Aud – she didn't know enough about my life in LA to know what Aud had meant to me. I just needed someone to talk to. I couldn't cry ... I thought I should be able to – Aud was my closest friend – but the tears just never came. So I called Louise thinking that talking to her might help take my mind off things. It didn't take long, however, before the conversation again turned in your direction.

"You're an idiot," she said once I'd finished describing our week together on-set and how you'd disappeared again at the end of our stretch. "That's all there is to it. You draw in dysfunctional lovers like flies to shit."

"Gee. Thanks," I said.

"It's true. Mark thinks so, too." Mark was Louise's new boyfriend with whom she'd already shared our family's history. Because this was the story of my life.

"I'm unlucky," I said.

"The Jews were unlucky, M______. You're a glutton for punishment."

"Did ... did you just compare my love life to the Holocaust?"

"Time. Everything's funnier in time."

"I don't think it works that –"

"You meet these guys who smile at you pretty and treat you real swell for a few minutes, and you go ahead and give them a blow job in the janitor's closet and what happens next? They walk all over you. Every. Single. Time."

"Not every single time," I said, defensively.

"Oh, yeah? Carl ..."

"... Was going through a rough patch with his family."

"He was living in his parents' basement."

"And they raised his rent."

"And he was forty."

"He ... Carl was trying real hard."

"Fine then. Mike."

"Realized he wasn't over his ex and wanted to wait a bit – so he could be sure we weren't just another rebound fling."

"How long is a bit?"

"I don't see how this has anything to do with –"

"How. Long."

"... Four years."

"Daniel."

"Okay, see, that wasn't his fault. His wife was –"

"Oh, just fucking kill me already."

"Fine. I have shit for radar. Is that what you're trying to tell me?"

"Yes. Yes, it is. And this isn't any different."

"It *is* different," I said to her, instantly regretting being so open about our situation in the first place.

"Because he'll tell you to go fuck a fence post if you call him by his real name? You're right, M______, that's pretty goddamn different."

"That's not what I meant."

"Please. By all means. *Educate me.*"

"He's ... there's more to him than he's willing to admit, okay? There's a lot of love and kindness in him. I see it. I know it's there. It's just ... it's buried. For the time being."

"For the time being," she repeated haughtily. I could practically hear her nose pointing to the sky.

"Exactly."

"And you want to be the one to dig it all up."

"I ... no ... I mean ... Damn it, Louise, I'm not a fixer."

"No," she said, practically choking out the syllable. "Absolutely not. Also not gullible, naive or living in a dream world."

"Maybe you don't know me as well as you think you do."

"M______, enough. Forget this Hollywood Wonderland bullshit. Come home. Come back to what's real."

"What for? There's nothing for me there."

And she paused then, rather suddenly, and I could hear it in the silence that followed, what she'd wanted to say but didn't: she was there, still. She was waiting for the day I'd had enough and would return to her, so we could be a family again.

She hung up without so much as a sigh.

††

Three weeks passed. Louise had tried calling me back a few times that night, but I just turned my phone off and went to bed. She called again a few days later and I let it go to voice mail.

It was mid-July and we were sharing a scene dressed as Russian lab techs in a spy thriller – 007 fodder, white lab coats and thick black-framed glasses for targets. My hair was done up in a tight bun, with two yellow pencils marking an *X* through the back. We were on set for just one day of shooting, followed by a callback a week and a day later. It was for the same film, but we'd been transformed into a different set of background expendables.

Our first day on set, disguised as lab techs, I flirted with you in my best attempt at a Russian accent. Smiled at you, catching the corner of your eye between takes, seductively tracing your shoulder with my fingertip when standing next to you – calling you only by the name you'd been given in the script. I left as soon as our day had wrapped, before you could react to my presence. At the end of our second scene together, this time as a pair of unfortunate background tourists in a studio stand-in for Berlin – recently bullet-riddled bystanders without so much as names, pasts or identities – we walked off set, hand in hand, without anyone to mourn us or inquire as to our wrong-place-wrong-time demise. This time I didn't try to tell you my name, didn't try to guess at yours, didn't for a second pretend we were anything more than we'd been on the page.

It worked – you caught on. You glimpsed complicity, tenderness, in the way I gently squeezed your hand, as if we'd been together for years with names we neither knew nor cared. It was thrilling.

That night we went back to the motel we'd shared as Richard and Eleanor. As soon as the door closed behind us you started touching me, running your hands over my outer layer. You bit my ear, chewed through the single-use sleeve of my patchwork European model while traffic hurtled by in the night. The walls were thin; there was no doubt others would hear us. I sucked in a breath and you grew hot to the touch. There were no lines for us to memorize – no character arcs, no narrative rise or fall. Show, don't tell: the sounds of feet scuffling together, rubbing against the starch-hard motel bedspread. That night you tore my body free from its sleeve and I continued to lie with you as her, as we had been on set, together, a fiction.

Act II

14. Zeitgeist

Posted: 01/20/2014

Douglas Mayberry, Marine Corps. Part of a convoy killed by a roadside bomb during the pre-credit sequence of *Child of Honour*. This weekend, I finally had a chance to see the performance so raved about on *Access Hollywood*. D_____ looked good up there, for the three minutes and twenty-seven seconds of screen time allotted to him and the other superfluous grunts. The scene was impeccably shot and staged, and utterly layered with pathos, setting up the audience for two hours of tears as the titular little boy struggled to find himself with only the vaguest memories of last year's best supporting actor as his dad.

Andreas Rain did have a point: D_____ wasn't top billed or anything, but damn if the camera didn't fall in love with him. He was barely more than a name and a body, and still he managed to pull so much out of his ass: wide, watery eyes that, as he lay dying on the side of the road, his insides half out of his body, looked like they were actually staring at whatever it was that existed on the other side of this world. In just seconds he effortlessly threw down against dear old best-supporting-actor dad who'd appear in flashbacks for the rest of the film and *still* wouldn't be remembered as strongly.

Seven hundred and sixty-four. And as an added bonus he succeeded, in a single calendar year, at dying onscreen alongside all four of last year's Oscar-winning actors and actresses. A dubious honour to which they're all thrilled, I'm sure.

Do you know who contacted me today, Douglas Mayberry? Ezra Cunting Oppenheim. It was a quick conversation. Actually, it wasn't so much a conversation as it was a fax with the words *cease and desist* underlined and emboldened at the top of the page, her signature at the bottom, the two *P*s looped together like a bow tie with legs. All told, it was a little gauche for my tastes – a few flower doodles and some sparkles and it prettied up nicely, covered all that nonsense about "attacks" against her client, and "cease this destructive and nefarious slander at once or we will be forced to take legal action."

Now, I know what you're thinking, dear readers: Who in their right mind sends a fax anymore? But at least I now know they're paying attention to me. Pardon me for a moment while I directly address the agent in the room: Fuck off, Ezra. Respect my rights, freedom of expression, blah-fucking-blah. I've said absolutely nothing slanderous or incriminating about your client. Don't believe me? Take a look through the archives. Go ahead, I'll wait. And I'll give you a shiny nickel if you can actually find his name anywhere in print.

Done? Great. Then let's take a moment and talk about *zeitgeist* (noun: *the spirit of a time or age*). See, D_____ and I, we're on the tip of it. It's certainly fair to assume neither one of us expected this to happen, but forces – and talkative, effusive directors – have dragged us into the spotlight. For my part, I never anticipated this invective would appear on the front page of Reddit; until ten days ago, I hadn't even glanced at the blog's stats. As it happens, this quiet little story of excoriation and retreat is averaging eight to ten thousand unique views a day. I'm not even bothering to read the comments section most days, because, as I'm sure you're aware, therein lies madness, racism, sexism, homophobia and every kind of degrading, demoralizing slander they have a word for – and a few they don't. Hell, I've lost track of just how many people have told me to hurry up and kill myself, even going so far as to offer up suggestions as to how. Like I haven't already thought of most of them, you rank fucking amateurs.

D_____, on the other hand, put himself in this position. I'm not talking about what shitty thing he said when a microphone was unexpectedly shoved in his face. No, I'm referring to him being there in the first place. Red carpets were never his thing – too many eyes, too much attention. I wonder: What in the world would ever have flipped his opinion on that?

It seems we both unintentionally courted the fame now bearing down upon us like an asteroid from outer space. My hands are red with spite; his, I'm assuming, have been tied by the very same pit bull that fights all his battles for him, desperately striving to increase his brand awareness. It's okay, though. D_____, I'm addressing you now: it's okay. Continue your vow of silence, or non-aggression, or whatever protective legalese Ezra's using to keep you to a short leash. I understand. I won't even hold it against you.

††

There are more holes in our shared past than days in a year. I've been digging around for answers about D_____ – about who he really is, or was – since our very first meeting. And in that time I've found impressively little. His life before he turned twenty-four, when given his first chance to die for a living, is a series of loose threads and narrative inconsistencies – a class photo here, a college transcript there (first-year psych – oh, the layers), but nothing substantial, nothing that says, "this person existed and here is the life they led."

Aud tried to give me a hand with some of the research early on. Mostly it consisted of me googling his name(s) while she fast-forwarded through the mess of films I'd torrented, watching – cackling – at every single one of D_____'s death scenes, the more gratuitous the better. Every now and then I'd glance up and see her on her laptop, sitting on the floor of my studio apartment, with both hands over her mouth to keep from bursting. "Look!" she said once, spinning the laptop around so that I could watch that scene from *Desert Decapitators on the Loose* where his character, Michael Steelwater, gets taken out by a maniac wielding a bo staff with motherfucking *chainsaws* attached at either end. Because that seemed practical to someone in the prop department, I'm sure. It wasn't new to me, but Aud was losing her shit at the really, super, ridiculously low-budget rubber head they'd made for D_____, and the way his body just erupted like an overripe tomato at the first touch from one of the blades.

"This is too fucking good," she said, over and over again. I'd seen it already, though. I'd seen all of it more than once and still knew so little. The less I've discovered about him through hours and hours of research, the more I've allowed my imagination to run feral. It wasn't long after I began this blog that I started stitching him a sleeve of his very own – a Jungian archetype of the type of childhood I imagined, eventually, would direct an individual to his specific line of work. I envisaged him as a quiet boy, soft-spoken, maybe a little unsure of himself. He was probably small for his age, too, a bit soft around the middle and bullied for it, or maybe he had a face tragically oozing with whiteheads. Mom and Dad loved him, but just enough, just that little bit more than "like." He wasn't their concert pianist or star quarterback or future brain surgeon. At parent-teacher night he was that most unfortunate of things: adequate. No trouble, no excitement and absolutely not a trace of ambition. His parents likely did what they could to spark the renaissance soul they prayed was inside, somewhere, nesting, but nothing took; his bedroom was a dystopian junkyard of dust-covered guitars, drum kits abandoned and stacked against the wall, the floor littered with acrylic paints and briefly toyed-with chemistry sets.

It was this sort of speculative attention to detail, which I employed in the making of every sleeve, that seized his thoughts as we lay in bed together for the second time, in the almost-blackness of our motel room, following our turn as doomed European tourists. As had happened previously, the flesh around my stomach and hips had loosened in the night, where he'd grabbed it, where there'd been friction. He toyed with a ripple of skin, smoothing it out over the hard, less-pliant surface beneath, like he was pushing his fingers through foundation clay, pausing with his thumb on a slight indentation in my flesh, right at the pelvis. Without looking at it, he asked what it was. It's the seam, I replied, where I'd stitched together the different skin samples. He lapsed suddenly into an uncomfortable silence, and I could tell from the soft, distant glare in his eyes that he was working something out, trying to decide if what I'd said had been a breach of character, of trust. When he finally spoke again, it was the gentle, almost nasal pitch of his true self that I'd heard only once before: "How many?"

"How many what?" I asked.

"Sources," he replied, tiptoeing with his fingers up the seam at my pelvis, stopping where it connected to another along my side, just above the waist.

"I'm not sure," I said. "However many I need. Sometimes I leave a sleeve whole; other times I pick and choose which parts to keep, to best suit the narrative."

"So it's like when you have a portrait that, when you go in close, you realize is actually a whole bunch of different images."

"A mosaic. Exactly."

I could see him quietly nodding in the dark as he listened, contemplating what I'd just revealed. While it was true that Eleanor had been a complete idea in and of herself, it was equally true that sleeves like hers did not often come around. In most cases, I'd been forced into crafting a pastiche from a wide array of influences: the limber arms of an eighteen-year-old Lithuanian gymnast studying political science at Vilnius University, vacationing in LA for the summer; the rough hands and fingerprints of a former member of the Ukrainian armed forces I met one night at a bar in Culver City; the scarred, hidden torso of a southern Californian socialite sitting alone in a bookstore, pretending to read a magazine, begging the world to leave her alone, just for a moment, just long enough for her to catch her breath. It usually took little more than a glance for me to parse the lives of the women whose skin I sheared from their bodies. I'd become a professional at stalking silently twenty or thirty steps behind a mark – close enough to keep my inspiration in view as I followed them home, but far enough away that I would not be seen were they to suddenly turn and look in my direction. Often I'd wait until they'd unlocked the door of their house or apartment and I'd come up from behind, wrap one hand around their mouth and the other around their waist and force them inside, kicking the door shut from the other side of the threshold. I'd push them to the ground, holding a chloroform-soaked rag over their faces while visually poring over their belongings, noting how they'd decorated their space, with pictures and colours and tchotchkes. I'd drink in the materials of their surroundings while opening each drawer in the kitchen, looking for a chef's knife or a decent non-serrated blade that wouldn't fray the edges of the tissue as I scalped and de-skinned what pieces I needed to complete the persona I'd already outlined in my head. I would use what they had on hand – plastic bins, discarded Amazon boxes, laundry and duffle bags lined with green trash bags or plastic tarps to prevent visible leakage, to transport them safely home where I could then transfer them into the solution I'd prepared. The inside of my fridge was almost barren of essentials: there were condiments, half-empty jars of pickles and peanut butter, while top to bottom the shelves were stacked with the United Colors of Benetton, sheared to the bone, organized by body part and Pantone swatch.

The more patchwork characters I pieced together for myself, the better I got at seeing the gaps where my aesthetic – my narrow, jagged self – poked through, and the more efficient I became at patching from a greater accumulation of sources, to obscure any discrepancies between the sleeve and what resided within. The process of piecing together a sleeve for D_____ was different, though, because beneath the nation state of ghosts populating his career is still only the barest assumption of a person – threads of detail and only just. And I couldn't very well hide what I didn't know. And with D_____, I never really knew much of anything at all. The sole individual in his life who likely knows anything concrete about him is Ezra, but she won't talk. She's his enabler in all this. He said as much to me that night – the last of our time together, when he shattered both my jaw and his unspoken promise to me.

††

So here we are. The ground rules have been laid out and introductions made. I know now, thanks to Ezra, that he's out there, hiding among my readers in plain sight. Well, D_____, you can tell your pit bull, the next time you see her, that she can push as hard as she wants but it isn't going to deter me from stating my case, because a man without an identity has no rights to self-preservation.

15. Commitment

Posted: 01/25/2014

We weren't a couple, not even in the broadest definition of the term. There was something real between us that we both had silently acknowledged; still we remained untethered to one another. It was brutal, confusing, knowing you were there, with me, but also not, like having a parasitic insect relentlessly gnawing on my brain stem but not actually doing any damage, not letting my mind wander too far into what might have been. Lord knows commitment was never once discussed. Over the weeks that followed the start of our ... the start of us, I tried to think of ways to bring it up, but the timing was never right; it never felt like it was something we could even begin to discuss.

I heard the soft click of the door as you exited the motel room on our second night together, early in the morning. You thought I was still asleep. I didn't want to say anything to you at the time; it was long past midnight and your carriage had already turned back into a pumpkin. I stayed in bed for another hour, in the cold, damp remains of our fantasy, until I felt chilled. Then, wrapping myself in the bedsheet, I zombied into the washroom. Flicked on the light there and was shocked by what I saw; staring back at me from inside the mirror above the sink was a police report personified. I stood up straight, turned to the left, to the right: the skin of my upper body was pale and elastic as if too little fabric had been stretched over too large a frame, while loose portions had collected like folded curtains around my midsection and the tops of my thighs, fingerprints pressed into the flesh like newsprint in Silly Putty; my hair had thinned, and the seams between the different types of skin were white and visible in a way they hadn't been before, like the spine of a paperback novel that had been cracked one too many times. When I reached up and massaged the right side of my face the skin around that eye shifted in a circular motion, revealing the increasingly fragile body within the sleeve – pale and red and aggravated. I reached around to the back of my head, to the almost invisible zipper beneath what was left of my hair, and started to claw my way free of the tarnished, loose sleeve. The flesh around the opening was dry and flaked apart in my hands, turning into confetti that coated the sink, the counter, the white-tiled floor of the washroom.

When all was said and done, what stared back at me from the mirror was an emaciated body thin enough to have been sleeved inside a waiflike figure; that smelled stale, like a pair of used gym socks lost at the bottom of an athletic bag – a narrow, hipless, nearly shapeless skeleton structure of thoughts and ideas upon which to build. I touched my almost non-existent chest, the hairs pressed down from sweat, and it hurt, like my bones had turned brittle while sheathed within my myriad sleeves, the muscles in my arms and legs all but evaporated, leaving behind only strings and sinew and the vaguest impression of a build.

††

I didn't know where you'd gone or when – if – you'd be back, so that afternoon I went ahead and checked out of the motel. My first thought was to head home, but that didn't feel right. Home was a walk-up in Culver City where several days' worth of work writing obituaries had backed up on me. That place felt like a piece from a different life, one that didn't quite fit the same as it once had; a plot thread tied to a character that no longer existed. What we'd done – what we'd had was ... it was fake and made up and a total fabrication, yet ... If I told you that, based on almost nothing real, the night we'd spent together seemed among the most authentic of my life, would you think that I'd lost my mind? Because I can't think of any other way to describe how I felt after checking out, not wanting to return to the life I had, which had started to feel like the dream and not the other way around. Though the character I'd dressed in for the night had come to an end, the sleeve now a collection of dried and crumpled paper stuffed at the bottom of my overnight bag, it was still too soon to return to what I'd been before. I felt momentarily outside of myself, adrift in a neon haze.

The next day, while standing in line at Starbucks, a woman I'd known for years came up and stood behind me. Her name was Joyce and she lived down the hall from me – we'd said our hellos every time we passed one another either leaving or coming home – but that afternoon, while standing side by side waiting for our Americanos, she wouldn't face me, or even acknowledge me; didn't smile or nod when I smiled and nodded. Our orders arrived at the same time, and she picked hers up, turned and looked straight through me as if I were a ghost.

††

You reappeared a week later as I was sitting on a concrete stoop outside the Starbucks at the Howard Hughes Center, drinking a latte and reading a by-the-numbers mystery novel I'd picked up from a discount table at a bookstore.

"Excuse me," you said, authoritatively.

I looked up, surprised. You were dressed in black, from jeans to leather duster. Best guess: Eastern European hit man or two-bit cyberpunk castoff for whom a sense of humour was a potentially expensive proposition. I'd soon learn your new identity: Guard 528491 of the Kurzweil Corporation's Galactic Prison franchise.

"This place isn't safe," you boomed. (Your baritone was impressive – not sure if I ever told you that.) "There are ... unsavoury people around."

To both sides I saw families shopping up and down the promenade, pushing strollers, holding hands, rocking cut-off jeans shorts and pastel polo tees. My stomach dropped to my knees then, unexpectedly: I was naked. You were there for me, and I had on only my original skin, still slightly raw from contact. My throat dried up and I didn't know what to say. As if aware of what I was feeling, you extended your hand, palm up.

"Come with me if you value your life."

I took your hand then and you pulled me to my feet. "I'm ... I'm not sure who I'm supposed to be."

"It'll be okay," you said. "Just take my hand. Stay close."

16. Zero Chance, Zero Escape

Posted: 01/25/2014

EXT: PAY BY THE HOUR MOTEL -- AFTERNOON

GUARD 528491 leads M_____ to a motel three blocks from an abandoned warehouse that had been gutted and remodelled inside to resemble a twenty-third century prison complex -- complete with all manner of unfurnished piping and electrical wiring.

M_____ (V.O.)

*You were a prison guard with a bar code tattooed on the back of your neck -- a number without a name, like they did in so many pre-*Matrix *dystopians that tried to prove how edgy and like* Neuromancer *or* Snow Crash *they could be without actually understanding what made either so iconic.*

(*Beat*)
Tomorrow you were scheduled to die, to be thrown over the railing of the prison's second floor and into a waiting sea of thugs and villains with genetically enhanced bodies and cybernetic limbs.

GUARD 528491 stops in front of ROOM 15 and inserts a key into the lock. He opens the door and M_____ follows him inside.

CUT TO:

INT: PAY BY THE HOUR MOTEL ROOM 15 -- AFTERNOON

GUARD 528491 walks over to the bed and sits down. At his feet is a BLACK DUFFLE BAG.

M_____ stands just inside the door, staring down at the BLACK DUFFLE BAG.

M_____

What's that?

GUARD 528491 pushes the BLACK DUFFLE BAG with his foot.

M_____ kneels down and hesitates briefly before opening the BLACK DUFFLE BAG.

M_____ (V.O.)

You wordlessly kicked the bag over to me. I glanced up and you were smiling the eager, almost childish smile of someone who knew, who just knew that they'd found the perfect Christmas gift -- smiling, but trying not to. Trying to remain stoic and militaristic. The top of the bag bulged and I could see a damp patch where blood had soaked through. I knew what was inside before I'd even unzipped.

Inside the BLACK DUFFLE BAG are the FLAYED SKINS of at least a dozen different women -- some full, some piecemeal. M_____ turns and COUGHS from the INTENSE STENCH within. Then reaches into the bag and pushes aside the SKINS at the top, noting the roughness of their edges.

M_____ (V.O.)

They were dry and at risk of becoming worthless -- I wanted to take them home right away, treat them, parse them as needed. Before I could, though, I took a moment to revel in ... surprise. At what he'd done, the gift he'd given. Had he done this before? Was there method to his acquisitions or were they just what had come around?

(Beat)

I smelled memories of a carnival -- a thick combination of cotton candy, hot dogs and manure; another slip of skin smelled like a dry cleaner's, like nothing it had worn had ever been laundered at home. Another produced almost no olfactory response beyond that of viscera; however, its texture was especially rough and without give, without pliability. Whoever had worn this last sleeve had spent a lifetime attempting to mask their origins, whatever they might've been, wherever and why.

(Beat)

The flaying was quick work by an obviously unsteady hand, but it didn't matter. There was enough material in the bag that I could put together whatever I needed for ... whoever I was supposed to be, now and for the foreseeable future.

(Beat)

When I looked up at you again, your excitement had dissipated and I caught you staring off into space.

GUARD 528491

(Unnerved)

That place is going to be the death of me. I know it. I just ... I'm sure of it.

M_____ (V.O.)

What was I supposed to say? I'd not seen the script -- I didn't know what sort of role I was meant to play, or if I was meant to play one at all. For all I knew you were a man married to his work with no life outside the prison. I was flying blind and quickly fished a life from the ether.

M_____ places a hand on GUARD 528491's chest.

M_____

(Concerned)

You can walk away from ... from that place.

GUARD 528491

I can't.

M_____

You can. I know it's difficult to accept, but --

GUARD 528491

The company ... if I leave my post, they'll come after me -- after us. There's nowhere to go, nowhere we can escape to.

M_____ sits on the bed next to GUARD 528491 and puts a hand to the bar code on his neck.

M_____

We can still try.

GUARD 528491

We won't make it.

M_____

What matters is that we give it our best shot.

GUARD 528491
They'll kill us. They'll kill *you*.

M_____
(Smiles)
Then we give them hell before we go.

M_____ leans in and KISSES GUARD 528491 on the lips.

17. The Best Stories Bleed Real Blood

Posted: 01/28/2014

It was fast becoming the norm, me waking up alone in motel rooms, feeling sunrise disoriented while I tried to remember where I was and how to get home again. As Guard 528491, he'd slipped out of the room at four in the morning to face his destiny head-on. I had pretended to be asleep, but still I felt it as he sat on the edge of the bed, the ancient mattress springs creaking beneath as he laboriously put on his boots. His character's impending doom sat heavily on his shoulders, forced his head to the ground in what could easily have been mistaken for either prayer or quiet resignation.

An hour after he left I got up and showered, still dressed in my best interpretation of our night together – in a patchwork of the skins he'd provided. He'd wept with me over the life he was scheduled to lose – the life that was never his to begin with. And while I was sitting down at a greasy spoon just up the street from the motel, getting a plate of runny scrambled eggs with carbon-black bacon and "freshly brewed" turpentine on the side, he was being unceremoniously torn to pieces by an escaping prison mob of futuristic cyber deviants. Running another forkful of egg through a glob of ketchup on the corner of the plate, the red and yellow and white mixing in a disconcertingly gory manner, I thought of dropping a twenty on the table and hurrying to the set, to be there for him when he needed me most. But I didn't. I knew enough to see that the skin I'd stitched together the night before, from the patterns he'd stolen for me – for us – had already started to wither from strain and lack of treatment; small cracks like pale winter lips had started to appear in the webbing between my fingers. It wouldn't take more than a scrub brush or a coarse towel to open an exit wound in this sleeve. To say nothing of my ability (or lack thereof) to break onto a closed set. I did the only thing I could think to do and went home.

††

I've asked myself on more than one occasion if what we had was really all that different from the relationship between a sex worker and a john. There was a sense of impropriety to the whole thing, starting from the moment he slid that duffle bag of skins over to me. It was akin to a sack full of money, and held an inherent degree of quiet accommodation that accompanies such ... transactions. Even if it was something I wanted, or thought I wanted; even if at that moment it was exciting, in the aftermath I struggled to tell the difference between the wear on my sleeve and that of my heart. But when I opened the bag and the thick, dense memories wafted out, filling the space between us, all my concerns and hesitations and reasoned arguments against just ... crashed to a halt. I stopped seeing the rendition of D_____ that appeared when he exited the makeup chair at the end of each day. In his place I saw, first and foremost, Charlie the Chin, who was sweet and funny and kind to me that day – the first I saw him die – and not at all the mysterious collection of half-promises he was turning out to be. In Charlie there was still the hope of something more. Like there always is at the start of something new. Maybe Charlie saw the me in Malorie and not the other way around. Maybe he, unlike so many others, saw my true face and all the others I wore and didn't need a caveat for any of it.

When I revealed this to my therapist at our session last week, she asked if in fact I felt like a sex worker, or if I'd simply felt wronged and was looking for something – a label – to secure myself.

"I don't think so," I said.

"Which part?" she asked, tapping her pen against the pad of paper she balanced on one knee. I wished she would stop. She talked so much about my obsessions, my idiosyncrasies, but right now it was all I could hear – that *tap tap tap* in groupings of three, like she had a waltz stuck in her head that she couldn't help but share.

"I'm not just looking to put a handle to this mess. I've better things to do than play name-my-psychosis."

"It's not necessarily a bad thing, M______. Putting a handle on things, as it were. That's part of what we're trying to accomplish here: isolating how you feel and condensing it into something small and manageable that might help you to better see the whole picture."

"But I've already seen it," I said. "I lived it. I'm still living it."

"Which is at the very core of your problem – you're still so deeply entrenched in the past that it has physically manifested right here, in your present. Biology makes up only one half of our health, you know. The key to lasting wellness is in caring equally for one's mind as one's body."

"I'm fine," I said, louder and more abruptly than I'd intended.

"You're not," she countered. "You're in deep, extended denial about your relationship with D_____. Otherwise we wouldn't still be discussing it more than a year after the final swing of the axe, for lack of better phrasing."

"I'm moving forward, just like you said to do. I'm writing about him now, not my past –"

"But you are."

"– and not about Dad or Mom or Louise, not anymore. This is about me and him and how he treated me."

"Which was like a sex worker."

"I ... No ... The sex was consensual."

"Prostitution often is consensual, M______, to a greater or lesser degree. The issue here is intimacy – trust – not consent. If you were to view the events of your time together as a series of transactions – that you accepted – and not perhaps the togetherness you sought, then what stage have you on which to argue your point? Why did you allow such things in the first place?"

"Because I was in love with him."

"No," she said, flatly, "you were in love with the *idea* of him."

"Is there a difference?"

"A monumental one."

"But no one's really who they say they are," I quickly said. "Everyone lies. Everyone exists as their best hope for themselves."

"If that's your belief then why try for intimacy in the first place? Isn't it by its nature more trouble than it's worth?"

"I don't ... I mean I'm not ..." I started feeling hot beneath the collar of my shirt. I reached up then and pinched the skin at the back of my neck, to allow it to breathe, and the dry, chalky feel of it reminded me I was trapped there, in her office, as myself.

She continued: "You're angry because while you initially got what you wanted from D_____, you quickly found out that, like blind love in every form, it wasn't all it was cracked up to be."

"That's not it," I said sullenly. She folded her arms across her chest, pen still in hand, ready – waiting for me to tear the head off some new scab at which she could pick and poke. "I wanted to play in new sandboxes with him, I genuinely did. That was exciting and everything, but still I wanted the impossible that really should not have been. And with practically anyone else probably wouldn't have been."

"Which was what?"

"For him to come home with *me* at the end of the day."

"Which brings me back to the question I asked when you first started writing your blog: What do you hope to accomplish through this? It isn't transparency. Look at you," she said, pointing accusingly to my hand still absently teasing the flesh at the back of my neck. I quickly dropped it to my lap. "You don't really want to strip yourself down – you're still too busy trying to hide beneath the stories and lives you've taken for yourself."

"They're mine," I said. "I earned them, every last one."

"You stole them."

"From people who didn't know what a good thing they had. Their lives, they were being wasted on boring people with zero ambition."

"That's not for you to decide!" She paused, cleared her throat, before continuing at a much calmer register. "In your entry from eight days ago, you called your blog an invective. A tirade, M_____, which leads me to believe the following: This was never about transparency. This is not – and has never been – about honesty, or about finding your truth. This blog is retribution of a sort, and you've chosen to rake both your bodies over the very same bed of coals. Why? What for?"

She waited then, for me to fill the space with enough silence that the session would simply draw to a close. Or maybe she was holding out hope that I would somehow choke myself with my own words.

"I'm trying to figure out what went wrong," I said, eventually.

"But when was it ever right?"

"When it was just the two of us."

"Except, M_____, it never was just the two of you. Isn't that what you've been telling me all this time? You were never you and he was never himself, either."

"No, that's – I didn't say that."

"What is it that you're trying to understand? Really?"

"... I think ... I need you to stop reading my blog."

"It's public material, M_____. You've opted to share it with the world."

"But not you."

"I'm part of the world. Why not me? Are you afraid I'll find out something you'll wish I hadn't?"

"No, but –"

"Because if you hope to get a handle on things, I need you to be completely honest with me."

"I am. I mean I have been."

"Then why are you afraid? What is it you're trying to find out?"

"I want to know if I mattered!"

Doctor None-of-Your-Business sat back in her seat. At first I thought she was surprised by my outburst, but then she smiled, slowly, slyly. Fucking *satisfyingly.* She waited patiently for me to continue.

"I want to know if I mattered," I repeated once I'd calmed down again. "I want ... I need to know if there was ever anything between us – anything real I mean – or if I've just been deluding myself this entire time."

"It wasn't a real relationship," Doctor None-of-Your-Business said, firmly. "It's time you admit this to yourself. What the two of you had ... It was a fiction."

"But it still hurt like it was real."

"The best stories always do."

18. Tragicomedy

Posted: 02/05/2014

If we, in fact, were a fiction, as Doctor None-of-Your-Business suggested, what type would it be exactly? Certain possibilities could be immediately eliminated: we weren't action or adventure; there was no science fiction or fantasy to what happened between us, when we were alone, no matter the pattern of the wallpaper. In a romance – most romances, anyway – there exists a certain degree of sympathy toward the plight of the two (usually) likeable leads. Suffice to say in this we were lacking. Hard. So humour me a moment. Let's see if we can figure this out by examining the elements of proper storytelling.

Plot: Lovers meet, fall for one another, fall into bed together, and our flower-petal-delicate protagonist (yours truly) is quickly swept up in a whirlwind series of escapades, sexcapades and misadventures – with the occasional flaying – predominantly flirtatious, sometimes physical in nature. The object of our hero's affection is more than a little bit fucked in the head, or is playing hard to get, or *is* hard to get because he really *is* fucked in the head, but our hero's cool with that because, as is well documented, love is blind, deaf and, on occasion, exceedingly stupid.

Character: You, me and an audience of nearly eight hundred part-time personality cut-outs. Not to mention dear, sweet, not-at-all-vindictive Ezra, and some roadside debris piled next to a signpost that read *friends and family*.

Also Aud.

And Louise.

Conflict: Man versus self ... versus self, versus self, versus self. To say you're your own worst enemy is about as dramatic an understatement as one can make. Each life of yours is usurped by the next as if you're *Highlander*-ing with yourself. Which seems all the more sad now that I've written it out.

Setting: Every motel in town with a by-the-hour rate and an undercover cop in the parking lot sipping scalding hot Dunkin' Donuts coffee, waiting for the kids in room two-zero-whatever to bust out the weed so he can get his chance to be the bad motherfucker he always knew he could be. They didn't notice us, though. Not at any motel we stopped at on our journey. We were as invisible as could be to anyone not paying direct attention.

Atmosphere: *Alice in Wonderland*–style surrealism – every scene, every interaction a reinvention of all that came before, with about as much narrative consistency as an acid trip. We set decorated with the best of them without ever picking up a saw. Well, not for wood, anyway.

Style: Impermanent. *Transient.*

We certainly weren't a tragedy. Effective tragedy requires consistency building toward an appropriately painful resolution. A tragedy is a snowball rolling downhill, accumulating shrapnel and broken pieces of rock, wood and dirt as it moves. The route we took was one of opposition, of removing those extraneous things – people – from our lives. Tragedy implies manipulation of one party by the other, but we were both of us liars – experts in the craft, you might say. Though I think, all things considered, you were in a league all your own. Together we embodied the worst traits of Norman Bates and Tom Ripley, of Verbal Kint and Evelyn Mulwray.

We weren't a tragedy. We also weren't action, adventure, romance or even remotely family friendly. We were a black comedy steeped in noir and dissolution.

Doctor None-of-Your-Business said the best stories are often painful, disconcerting; that they don't feel good when they're happening because they're not – not in the least. They're abusive and interrogative, and at the end of it all, if done right, if handled with even an ounce of truth, you're lucky to be left with anything concrete to hold onto.

And that swirling, nauseating uncertainty that comes after? When the story's done and you're left looking back on all that shit and heartache piled up in your wake like debris from a hurricane? That's reality – that's catharsis fucking with you. It's like pride, but without.

19. A Shark in Snake's Clothing

Posted: 02/08/2014

It was August, and more than a dozen one- or two-day roles later, that we again had the opportunity to share a scene. In it, we were strangers on the set of a Civil War epic. There were no spoken lines between us, no seconds together on film; we were connected only briefly as our eyes locked from across the town square. I thought, for a second, I noticed you giving me the shortest of out-of-character grins, but I had no way of being sure. I was the neglected wife of a general for the North; you were a prisoner from the South accused of stealing into an encampment with a party of five others, cold and starving and in urgent need of medical attention. In your desperation, you and your accomplices slaughtered more than a dozen soldiers while they slept for what little food and money they had on their persons. In our scene together, I watched, standing shoulder to shoulder with the rest of the town, as the six of you were lined up against a wall and simultaneously executed for your crimes. The gunshots echoed sonorously. Still, they seemed somewhat muffled. Blanks sounded so close to actual rounds yet ... not, I thought, standing there, watching, pretending to be broken hearted, knowing that they'd amplify the report in post. You died then, chest blown open, dressed in filthy, soiled rags and slumped over the body of one of your comrades-in-arms. We remained silent, still, and then slowly dispersed, leaving the executioners to tend to their mess.

That night, as I waited for you, I met a guided missile made to look like a woman. She was short and stout, barrel-chested, her hair tied back so tight her face looked like wet fabric draped over a rock to dry. She wore a bright pink chiffon jacket with a lime-green trim – one of those straight-out-of-the-'80s combinations so bright it managed to offend even the legally blind – with gold and plastic technicolour bracelets clattering together on both forearms. She was waiting for me outside of makeup, stopped me mid-step and asked for my name. I answered, and she gave me a baking-soda smile in return.

"Ezra Oppenheim," she said, all teeth and no pucker. Her voice was that uncomfortable grey area between high pitch and gravelly, like a sixty-year-old two-pack-a-day smoker who never went through puberty. Or like late-model Joan Rivers high on helium. "Might we have a word?"

"Umm ..."

"It's all right," she said. "He'll be a while still. It sometimes takes a bit of elbow grease to get the blood out of his hair."

"Wait, you know –"

Without skipping a beat, she palmed me a one-by-three card with bevelled edges, her name emblazoned on the surface like a decorative scar: EZRA OPPENHEIM – TALENT.

"I don't understand," I said. "I don't really need an agent."

"Sweetie pie, I don't give a shit about that. I'm here to talk to you about your choice in men."

My choice in – "I'm sorry ... but how is that any business of yours?"

She grabbed me by the bicep and quickly led me away from set, before you could reappear. "Walk with me."

I don't have to tell you Ezra's little more than a brick through a window – a thin pencil sketch of greed, bluster and vermouth. She doesn't pretend to be nice, doesn't mince words and never holds anything back. Strange as it is, though, you need her. She's your fulcrum of normalcy – the one person in your life you trust, on whom you can count to carve a path through all your crap without needing or wanting anything but for you to do your job and make her rich. It's a match made in heaven, if heaven were a wooden slat wall with a glory hole in it. How did she know who I was, I wondered in the back of my brain. Simple: you'd told her; you'd confided in her as if she were your mother. With Ezra in the picture, I never even had a chance.

"You're my own personal X factor," she said, leading me to the far end of the building. "You're mucking up the works, honey, and I don't like that – not one bit."

"I don't know what you're talking about," I said, truthfully.

"And the worst part is," she said as she snare-drum smacked a piece of nicotine gum, "that you're so fucking green you don't even see it."

"Please, don't hold back. Tell me what's really on your mind."

She raised a wrinkled, spray-tanned finger to my nose. "Don't you get snotty with me. I'll have you strung up by your ankles and left to rot."

"Such a charmer you are."

"Charm's for whores and producers, honey, and all too often they're one and the same."

"All right," I said, and pivoted in front of Ezra, wrestling free from her grip. "Get on with it then. What do you want with me?"

Ezra glanced over her shoulder, back across the set to where you were being cleaned up and made current again. "You're not the first, you know," she said. "Others have tried to be with him. It never works. It can't – it won't. It's better you know this now so you're not surprised in a week or a month or five when he up and vanishes like a cardinal's finger up a choirboy's ass." She exhaled, pinched the bridge of her nose, jangling one row of bracelets. It all seemed so dramatic, so ... intentional. Like she was putting on a show. Or was a show – she'd lived this hustle for so long she didn't know how to turn it off. "I've swept up after him before and I'm prepared to do it again, but I thought I'd try to talk some sense into you first. See if I couldn't get you to look at things with a clear head and a cold heart."

"You said there've been others ..."

"Is there a question in that statement?"

"A ... yes, I suppose."

"Suppose nothing. For god's sake, be a – Grow a pair. Speak up."

"What happened the other times?" I asked, nervously, as if I were giving a book report and my teacher was standing just two feet away, one arm stiff at her side while the other taps a wooden ruler against her pleated thigh.

Ezra bit the nail of her left index finger. It looked rough, with dried blood around the edges – one dead soldier out of ten. She severed the half moon, crudely spitting it to the ground. "I'm all he has," she said, ignoring the question. "And don't think for a second I don't see the angle you're pulling."

"Angle? What angle? What am I doing that's so wrong? How do you even know who I am?"

She leaned in close, exuding an odour of Red Bull and nail polish remover. "Do you think I'm stupid? Listen, honey, and listen well: I am a goddamn hawk – my eyes are on every frame of every job he's ever done. I know you've been tracking his movements. Maybe you've got friends on other sets keeping tabs on him, or you're watching the trades, keeping your eyes on his where's, what's and the other two."

"Three."

"Three?"

"There are five *W*s."

Ezra stared blankly.

"... Sometimes how, too."

"The fuck I care? Look, you've got yourself a fine career doing –" she gestured with her hand, limp and dismissive "– whatever it is you do. No one's telling you to walk away from that. I'm just warning you ... however you've managed to catch his interest, it won't last. He can't sit still for long – he doesn't have it in him."

And there it was: the truth, as blunt and menacing as only Ezra knew how to be. For as good as we were at lying about ourselves, D_____, we had nothing on Ezra's ability to slice open a person's throat with only brutal and honest facts. At first I thought she was just jealous; without meaning to, I'd become the "other" in your amicable and very profitable twosome, and she was none too thrilled about the competition. But her doom-and-gloom outlook was a little too stay-away-from-my-boyfriend-bitch for it to be just about business. She loved you, I remember thinking at the time, but she knew, for probably too many reasons to count, that it couldn't and wouldn't have worked between you. This was an if-I-can't-have-him-no-one-can scenario – how very high school of her.

It was over time, though, that it became clear she was more interested in being like your mother than your lover. After all, you were her golden goose; she saw more action – and more dividends – from your incomparable ability to roll over onto a hand grenade than probably any other client on her roster. The more work you got, the fewer children she probably had to keep chained to the wall in her pantry. When she came to me with sweet-granny threats and jabs to my self-confidence, it wasn't cruelty that motivated her but "proactive risk assessment" – she was protecting her retirement investment.

"Look," she said, temporarily dropping her vitriol for sugar-free sweetener, "you seem like a nice kid, but D_____ isn't made for love. He's a looker, sure, and this ... proclivity of his, it might seem like a rush at first but it won't last. You'd do well to remember: his eyes need to be on the prize at all times. The last time he allowed himself to get tangled up with someone like you –"

"The hell do you mean, 'someone like me'?"

"– they broke his heart, and he was so torn up about it he skipped out on a month's worth of work, started begging me to find him something friendlier, something where he could keep his insides inside of him. He started to doubt what he did – which he does better than anyone, I'll have you know. It broke my heart to see it. Took some hard work and convincing before he was made right again, and I am not going to let anything – or anyone – mess that up."

She paused, sighed. "He doesn't 'do' the whole 'people' thing. Not for long. He says he wants it, sure. He probably wants what any of us want out of love – someone to be there when the money comes in but also when you've got your head in a toilet."

"Real great relationship goals you've got there."

"He wants it," she continued, "but he can't have it. It doesn't work for him. He can't keep dying if he's lost his reason to live."

I honestly had no idea how to respond to any of what she'd just said. I couldn't even process it, not really.

"What is it?" she asked, and I realized I'd been staring off into space. "Why put yourself through all this just to be with him?"

If she'd asked Louise this, my sister would have said I was a naive masochist who didn't know any better – an unrealistic dreamer who did what I could to make my life as hard as possible. Aud would've said the same – that I liked to make things difficult for myself. And that I was probably as interested in D_____'s ability to die and be reborn as was Ezra, albeit for very different reasons. But there and then, as your agent detailed, in vague terms, your myriad shortcomings, I thought of all the ways I'd never been enough for the people in my life – of the role I was expected to occupy: the strong one, the provider; of the things I should have been, that my parents *wished* I had been – and of all the things I could still be with you.

"Because he fascinates me," I said, not telling her all that I was thinking. "Because I'm like him, more than you know. And I care for him."

"You care for him," said Ezra, "because you think he's something more than he is. But he's not." Her voice dripped with bitterness and pity. "He's a cipher, built for a singular purpose, and that's all he'll ever be."

And you know something, Ezra? You were right. You're a callous, unsentimental cunt, but you were right.

20. Venom

Posted: 03/01/2014

Two weeks ago, on a Tuesday night around nine-thirty, I saw a woman standing in the produce section at the Pavilions on Jefferson Boulevard with a melon balanced in the palm of each hand, carefully guesstimating the difference in weight between the two items. I didn't know who she was; I'd never seen her before, but once I noticed her it was impossible for me to look away. She was maybe five nine, five ten, two-twenty at least – as perfect an hourglass as I've ever seen, with ample hips and a soft, pliant midsection. Her face was teakettle-round and gentle, like something out of a nursery rhyme. This woman, in her quiet, fallow shade, moved elegantly through the aisles, every ten or fifteen paces stopping and checking the list she'd written on her phone, to make sure there was nothing she was forgetting. I stayed far enough behind her that she wouldn't notice me, watching her from neighbouring aisles and through gaps between products on shelves. When she made her way to one of the open checkout lines, I quickly redirected my attention to why I was there in the first place: I pocketed a couple of granola bars and a small bottle of mouthwash – just what I could stuff into the lining of my coat – and hurried for the exit.

Standing beneath a burnt-out street light at the far end of the Pavilions' parking lot I took two large swigs of mouthwash, to get rid of the dense film of vomit that had coated my tongue and the back of my throat for the better part of the day. The combination of the two tastes was like mint-flavoured vinegar, though not as pleasant.

It's getting harder and harder these days to keep my head above the tide. The last paying job I'd had was more than two months ago – a bit of background work in a hospital drama; the *Times* let me go after I'd missed a deadline for the third time in a row. I tried to tell them it wasn't my fault – that I wasn't feeling well and was waiting on my insurance to come through. Doctor None-of-Your-Business informed me that I couldn't come back and talk to her until I'd gone and seen a medical professional, put back on a few pounds, got the help she claimed I so desperately needed. Little did she know: I tried to get help, but they turned me away at the hospital – I had no money, and they discovered that my passport was fake when they tried to run it through their system. Far as they were concerned, I didn't exist – they even threatened to call the cops on me.

I'd never before been asked to show so much ID. Figured when I gave them my driver's licence that would've been enough, but no, they said. They needed something more. They asked for a passport, a credit card and a utility bill, saying they needed to know I was who I said I was. I'd thought something like this might happen, Ezra, that you'd make some calls, use whatever pull you still had to try and silence me. That you'd use what I'd revealed on this blog, namely my illegal status, against me. I wouldn't have put so much information out there if I hadn't been willing to deal with the consequences. I just didn't expect it would happen so fast. The hospital asked if there was someone they could call on my behalf, even as they were motioning for security to come and, I don't know, take me to a holding room or something, but I left quickly and without giving them my real name – any of them.

The curvaceous woman stepped out of Pavilions a few minutes later. I noted the make and model of her car, and her licence plate, memorized them as she lined her bags of groceries in a tidy row on the back seat.

I kept an eye on the lot, which was just a short walk from my apartment, searching row by row for her car every time I passed by. Three days later she was back, and this time I'd come prepared. Earlier that afternoon I'd slipped into a weathered skin I'd harvested two summers ago – Alaina. She was special to me. D_____ liked to get his hands all knotted up in her curly strawberry-blond hair when he pulled her – my – face toward his. I pleaded with him to stop every time he did that, said he'd damage the sleeve if he wasn't careful, but I was speaking in subtitles and he couldn't be bothered to read.

Alaina was coming apart at the seams. I'd patched her with swatches of Charlotte from Gainesville and Claire from Portland – dancers, both, limber, their legs like lithe collections of rubber bands. Alaina was, once upon a time, one of my better sleeves, but her days were numbered. This woman, though, the one I'd seen just a few days earlier, she had the look of soft maple cream, unscathed, unburdened by the world around her. She looked bright and healthy in a way my own skin hadn't in months, possibly years. Hers was a skin I could take whole cloth, like Eleanor's, and be protected inside. I waited for her to enter the store and collect her items again. When I next saw her, through the large panel windows at the front of the store, standing in the checkout line, getting ready to come outside again, I pulled a cutthroat razor from my inside jacket pocket and started walking toward her parked car. I arrived there at the same time as the abundant would-be sleeve in front of me. She held her two bags of groceries in one hand and reached for the rear passenger door of her car with the other.

"Here, let me help you," I said, rushing over to her, taking the bags from her hand so she could get at her keys. The bags were like weight plates cradled in my arms, which had shrunk and were far weaker than I'd realized. I was glad to be hidden in clothes too big for my frame, lest my increasingly wiry appearance be cause for alarm.

"Thank you so much!" she said. Her voice was melodic. She quickly unlocked the back door and opened it. I could feel my body beginning to tremble from the weight in my arms. "I got it," she said, taking the first bag from me and placing it on the back seat. She took the second bag from me then, and turned and offered her thanks, and I slashed out with the razor, cutting a small red canyon across the palm of her hand. She shrieked and fell against her car. I swiped again, shredding her blouse just above the elbow. She clutched herself and slid to the ground. I was getting dizzy, reckless with my motions; the blade shook like a feather in my hand. I tried to steady myself, to start the incision proper at her side, right above the hip, where I could take it all the way around. She whimpered, begged, asked me why, what did she do? The closer I got to her, though, the more I smelled it – something I hadn't smelled in any of the others: crackers and apple juice and cheese sandwiches with the crusts cut off. These scents and more – of children, of an entire family – exhaled from the cut on her hand and instantly I tasted bile like lemon rind and bitter almonds climbing up my esophagus, touching my tongue, the backs of my teeth, and I ran.

21. Because Dying's a Bitch, That's Why

Posted: 03/15/2014

"It isn't the readership that's depressing," I slurred the other night over the phone to Doctor None-of-Your-Business – her home number, not her office. She'd given it to me on our sixth session, in case of emergencies. "It's that in all these emails and comments that keep coming in, I've still not heard from the two people I want to hear from most of all." I started laughing, coughing into the receiver. "Maybe you were right about this – it's all just a cry for attention."

"M______, I appreciate that you're hurting, but we can't be talking about this right now."

"You said if I needed help that I could call you."

"Yes, and I promised I'd find someone for you. Someone ... more equipped to help get you over this hump."

"You mean someone I can afford."

"..."

"But I want to talk to you, not some public health flunky just out of psych school."

"Please, we've been over this. You sound ... you don't sound well."

"Is it about your chin? I didn't mean anything by the Witherspoon comment."

"M______, it's not –"

"I'll go back and delete it. I'll leave you out of the blog from now on – from here to the end, no more posting our sessions. Scout's honour."

"I won't do this over the phone."

"Then I'll come in again. When have you got an opening?"

"... Are you working yet? Have you gotten your finances sorted out?"

"No. But ... No. Fuck it – I'll figure something out."

"M______, stop. You need to go home. You need help I can't provide. What you're doing ... You're only hurting yourself now. Call Louise. Talk to her. Get taken care of before it's too late."

"But ... but we're not done here. There's still more to do!"

"Goodbye, M______, and good luck."

††

NyQuil and Tylenol 3 on an empty stomach. That's my excuse. Doc, if you're still by some chance reading this, I'm sorry for my behaviour. For ... all of it, really. I know it's not much, but it's the truth. And I'm all about the truth these days.

Ezra, I *know* you care about the truth more than anyone. So where was it we left off? Right. You telling me D_____ wasn't what I thought he'd be, and that he never would be. But that was then, and despite maybe your better instincts, it was honest; it would seem now you're more concerned with keeping whatever you can under the rug. I'm happy to see you've at least graduated from faxes to email, but you still don't have a leg to threaten on. You're between a rock and a bear trap: you want to protect your client's identity(ies) and your own from being towed through the mud any more than they have already been, but you can't come right out and claim it's all lies and untruths without unintentionally lending credence to at least some of what I've said. Because this is the Internet, bitch, and you know as well as I do that the court of public obsession won't allow this blog a quick death – not with the kind of numbers I'm pulling in. No, you might as well admit we're bunk mates: you're in this for the long haul.

I know what you'll do next, though. You'll try to get me on the basis of a threat. You'll call up your crack team of lawyers, if you have one, and they'll advise you to come after me with another cease and desist order – on formal letterhead this time – on the grounds that I'm attacking you and your client's character. It won't work, though – you struck first, Ezra, and you'd do well to remember that. Until you fired that warning fax across my bow I'd left your name out of this. But go ahead and give me your best shot. I'm not afraid of you or D_____. You see, that's the beautiful thing about dying – that whole "fear" thing starts to take a back seat to everything else.

Was that the "sensitive information" you threatened in your last email to make public? That you absolutely could not have acquired through legal means? That I'm dying? Oh, I'm sorry, I forgot. No threats. Not here. Not between us pals. We're better than that, aren't we? What I want to know is, what was your play? A vote of no confidence? *Please, pay no attention, ladies and gentlemen of the Internet, to the vulgar, delusional ramblings of a has-been who never was. Just another poor soul unlucky in love, and in life, doing their part to drag down a good, honest, hard-working silhouette of a dead man.*

Ezra, you fool. That's my ace in the hole. It's true: I'm dying. I've got a sick mind and an even sicker heart. Trembling bowels, pathetic, whimpering lungs and an appendix that wants to vacate my toxic interior. Oh, and a tumour growing over the left side of my brain like a cartoon storm cloud that follows me everywhere I go. That's the big one, I suppose. It's the malignant fucking tent the rest of the shit huddles beneath to keep warm.

Right now, Ezra, I've got the best of both worlds working in my favour: nothing to hide, and nothing to lose.

††

I've been working on this entry for two days now. But whenever I sit down at my computer to write I start to feel sick again. Last week, fittingly enough, was the anniversary of Dad's death. He's been gone half my life, and now, when I wake up in agonizing pain in the middle of the night, clutching both sides of my head and dry heaving myself to exhaustion, it's almost like he never left at all. It's like he gave me one last gift – one thing he could be sure I'd have to wear like he did. Now when I put on one of the few sleeves I still have that's in one piece, even the smallest are too spacious for what little is left on my bones and I'm forced, too often for my liking, to see the rejected framework of what lies beneath. The hipless, breastless, shapeless shell of a never was or would be.

You know the fuckiest punchline of them all? It's this thing I learned back when I was in therapy in high school, about my anorexic eating habits. It's about control – about taking hold of at least one facet of your life, when all else seems as if it's spiralling out of control, and making it yours. Making your body a thing that *you* control, and not the other way around. Whenever I've been at a lower, more dangerous weight, it's been because the world around me seemed like something I couldn't touch. Now I've got this godforsaken cancer eating away at my brain and body, doing the work of the eating disorder for me, and I can't keep anything down to save my life. The one fucking thing I felt like I had any control over and I don't even have that anymore.

But I still have this story.

While Dad's been gone now sixteen years, it's only been about a year and a half since Mom died. I'd been ignoring Louise's calls for some time – since the last time she and I talked and the conversation, once more, dipped into my dating history. She'd said I'd been living in a dream world. It stung more than I was willing to admit. She tried periodically to get hold of me after that, giving up after a couple of weeks of no response. However, two days after meeting Ezra for the first time, while I was sitting in a Barnes & Noble tapping my pen against a blank notebook page, Louise called again. This time she left a message on my voice mail, immediately following with a text: *Listen. Please. It's important.* I was about to play the message when I spied a woman in her mid-thirties coming around the end of the aisle, her fingers tripping across book spines on the shelf in front of her – Palahniuk to Priest – as she searched for something she thought would be worth the investment. She looked Mediterranean; she had dark olive skin and long black hair, very fine, that extended several inches past her shoulder blades. She was wearing a cropped black T-shirt of a band I'd never heard of. The skin around her waist was taut, stretched across a muscular midsection. It was perfect in its almost impossibly firm appearance, and was exactly what I needed to finish a partially completed design that had been draped for weeks over the small table in my kitchenette. You would have loved it, D_____; I was stitching a dead ringer for your *You Can't Go Home Again* co-star, the one you stepped in front of a bullet for during the opening credits. At the time I thought it'd be all kinds of romantic.

Upon seeing that woman, I forgot all about Louise and her message. I closed my still-empty notepad and stood up from my seat, slipping quietly down an adjacent aisle from which I could watch as my target gave up her search for something interesting to read and headed instead for the exit. I followed.

Louise called again the very next day, while I was busy fitting my newly acquired skin swatch into the existing pattern, getting ready to stitch it all together and complete the new sleeve. I contemplated letting it go to voice mail, but decided on the last ring to pick up.

"You self-centred motherfucker," she said before I'd even had a chance to speak.

"Hello to you, too, sunshine."

"I've had your back all these years, I've been there for you through literally everything – even when Mom and Dad weren't – and this is how you repay me? I said it was important, M______. I said it was important and still you bailed."

"I'm sorry," I said, just then remembering her text from the previous day. "I got distracted."

"You got distracted?"

"You're repeating what I said. Again. You do this quite a bit."

"Well fuck you, here's something new: Mom's dead."

"What?"

"Yeah. Yesterday. You know, when I fucking called you the first fucking time."

"How? What happened?"

"Oh, now you care?"

"Louise," I said, calm as I could manage, "stop. I'm asking. I care."

She huffed loudly. I waited in silence for more than half a minute. "I get it, you know," she said, starting up again. "Why you left. I never doubted for a second your reasons. But just because you've got this great and complicated new life in LA doesn't mean we stopped existing up here."

"I don't know why you're so pissed," I said, suddenly frustrated that she was taking her anger out on me. "Mom never wanted me around. Why does it matter whether I was there or not?"

"Because *I* need help with this, okay? You ever think maybe that things haven't been so great up here? She barely left the house after Dad died. Just took her pills and shut the blinds and that was it. You needed to go, and I get that, I do, and I don't begrudge you that. But I couldn't. I was stuck here looking after her, because there wasn't anybody else. I changed her, and washed her, and ... and now she's gone. Heart attack in the middle of the night."

"Well ding-dong, then – move on with your life."

Louise fell silent again. "I don't believe it. I don't believe it. You're not the least bit upset by this, are you?"

"Should I be? *She didn't want me*, Lou. She wanted you. She made that perfectly clear every time she glossed over all your fuck-ups and sob stories while mine were ripe for retelling to anyone who'd listen."

Which was always how it had been. Dad might've been the one to really voice his disappointment in me, but Mom never disagreed with him. She never once came to my defence. She cared to the extent that she could – she sought help when she saw that I was sliding weight-wise – but it was never free; there was always an emotional surcharge to her actions, a debt I would need to pay. Like when I had to listen to her on the drive back from the doctor's office, saying, "You've put me through so much, do you not see that? Do you not get it? Is this all a game to you?" That was her favourite phrase. She brought it out all the time, like when shit went down with the yearbook committee: "Is this all a game to you? These are people you're hurting, M______!".

I'd not lived up to either of their expectations, that much was clear. And when Dad was gone, when it was just Mom, I was there to remind her all the more of what she'd lost.

"Yeah, and now I get to do all the final arrangements," Louise snapped.

"Well, you did get the better grades."

"For fuck's sake, M______."

"Why are you making this such a big deal? Just shove her in a pine box and send her out to sea."

"Fuck you!" she screamed. She was crying – I could hear the glass in her voice spiderwebbing from the centre out. I tried to think of something to say, some last-minute barb I could stick her with, to tell her to get her shit together and get on with living the life she wanted to live – that it wasn't my problem she felt some ridiculous lingering obligation to a woman who'd never treated me as anything more than an obstacle – but she hung up on me.

It's a strange thing, smart phones. You just push a button and the other person disappears. There's no heightened emotion from slamming down the receiver, no loud smash as it's thrown up against a wall. The other end just goes dead, cuts to black and you're done.

††

Louise Farris (1972–2012) was a kind and loving sister who grew up to be a doormat. And a bit of a snob. And fuck your business yoga pants. She is survived by her boyfriend, Mark, who continues to smile and nod and pretend like he matters.

Also, please don't throw out my movie box.

22. E-X-P-L-O-D-E.

Posted: 03/21/2014

> **ex•plode** /ik splod/ (**-plod•ed**, **-plod•ing**, **-plodes**) *v* **1.** *vti* **BLOW UP OR BURST** to blow up or burst with a sudden release of chemical or nuclear energy and a loud noise, or cause something to blow up or burst in this way **2.** *vti* **BURST OR SHATTER** to burst like a bomb or shatter into many pieces, or cause something to do this **3.** *vi* **EXPRESS EMOTION** to give vent to an emotion, suddenly or violently **4.** *vi* **INCREASE DRAMATICALLY** to increase suddenly in extent or severity in an uncontrolled way **5.** *vi* **PRODUCE VIVID DISPLAY** to produce a vivid, often sudden display of light or colour **6.** *vi* **APPEAR SUDDENLY** to appear, start or move suddenly and forcefully. To become a star. To *be* somebody.

It's what they use to describe that improbable scenario of unexpected stardom: He or she *exploded* onto the scene; so-and-so was walking their dog one day, or taking their kid to school, or waiting tables at IHOP, when the right pair of eyes passed over them at the *exact* perfect time. Suddenly they were whisked away by the steady hand of a strapping, young, late-twenties European import with proto-'80s sensibilities and an unhealthy admiration for the works of Stanley Kubrick or Martin Scorsese or Francis Ford Coppola. *You're gonna be a star*, they'd parrot. *Name in lights, Oscars out the ass, all your dreams and desires come true.*

Except it never happened like that. Not really.

By the end of that summer I'd stopped searching for my own work, for my own chance to explode onto the scene – any scene – and started following D_____ across the country. It was handled quietly at first – he'd leave a note or something with the details of the next shoot, smile a "see you later" at me and I'd find my way to him, ready with a selection of sleeves I'd be able to slip into in the heat of the moment. Gradually he started giving me more to go on. He'd photocopy certain pages of the script – his pages – and leave them in an envelope on the pillow next to my head in whatever hotel or motel room we were staying in; he never took me back to his place (if he even had a place), never wanted to come back to mine. I'd remain asleep, or pretend to be sleeping, even if he knew I was really awake. I was getting used to our routine: he'd leave; sometimes I'd cover the bill, sometimes he'd get it; and then I'd go home, or to a gas station bathroom somewhere with my wardrobe to prepare. Then I'd tuck my lengthening hair under a mesh wig cap and strip off all my clothes before pulling out the rolling suitcase I took with me on each of these trips. Inside were several carefully folded garment bags containing individual sleeves, as well as some needles and thread, a handful of cloth rags and a couple of sealed jars of the treatment solution. Once I knew where I was headed next and what I needed in order to fill in the off-script blanks of his life, I would select the appropriate sleeve and lay it out on the nearest flat surface, carefully treat it, stitch whatever threading had come undone or whatever wounds had opened in transit and step inside whoever it was I was supposed to be.

When we slept together, sometimes the sleeves got so damaged they couldn't be repaired. Sometimes I pushed things too far, let them go untreated for too long, and they fell apart with him on top of me, grinding both me and what remained of the skin I'd worn that day into the bedspread. The next day I'd make sure to clean up all that I could, to not leave any evidence of our lovemaking for housekeeping to find, for fear of what they might think. I went through more sleeves during this time than at any other. They did their job, though.

And I was whoever I was supposed to be.

I was whoever he needed me to be.

23. What Happens in Vegas ...

Posted: 03/21/2014

INT: BELLAGIO RESORT & CASINO / PETROSSIAN BAR -- LATE NIGHT

SARAH (37-year-old White female) squeezes the arm of her companion, BRILL (38-year-old White male). The two of them cozy up to one another on one side of the round table in one of the far corners of the lounge.

On the other side of the table sit ALEX (44-year-old White male) and his wife, SILVANA (30-year-old White female). They are sitting with a small gap between them, their hands clasped together in the space left on the seat.

M_____ (V.O.)

It was September and we were between

back-to-back shoots in Las Vegas. You'd taken me out for dinner and drinks on the strip. We were, for the moment, Alex and Silvana Irvine: you, a door-to-door insurance salesman; me, a long-limbed Sicilian-American mix in a pale pink slip with long black-brown hair curled halfway down my back. We were husband and wife on our first vacation in years, coming all the way down from Grand Forks, North Dakota, to see the lights and play some slots.

SARAH

(Laughing)

You guys are a riot! I just can't believe we haven't met before now.

SILVANA (V.O.)

That was Sarah. We bumped into her and her husband, Brill, earlier in the evening, while out on the strip, then again, in the lobby of the Bellagio, after we'd finished dinner.

(Beat)

They asked if we wanted a drink. You didn't even hesitate before saying yes.

SILVANA smiles at SARAH on the other side of the table and sips from her MARTINI.

SILVANA

It's a pretty big world out there. I bet there are all kinds of people you haven't met yet.

SARAH shakes her head.

SARAH

Oh, don't give me that! I don't want to hear it.

SARAH wags her index finger at ALEX and SILVANA.

SARAH (Cont.)

You two ... You're a pair of aces is what you are. This wasn't chance -- I don't believe in all that ... that right-place-right-time garbage. This was fate.

BRILL condescendingly pats SARAH'S thigh.

BRILL

(Smiling awkwardly)

Sarah's a big believer in the universe's grand plan for us all.

SILVANA (V.O.)

Listening to Brill was like witnessing a parent trying to explain away their child's eccentricities -- Oh, that rambunctious lunatic of mine, she says the craziest things.

(Beat)

But they were still very much in love with one another. That much was clear, right from the start. They'd been together seven years and each still stared at the other as if they'd been dating for less than a month.

SARAH turns and slaps BRILL'S wrist.

SARAH

Oh, hush up, you.

SARAH turns back to ALEX and SILVANA.

SARAH (Cont.)

Brill doesn't see the beauty in this world. All he sees is fluke and happenstance. Nothing but a world of potential and possibilities. That just ... it feels so cold to me.

ALEX reaches forward, picks up his MARTINI GLASS and twists it by the neck. He stares at the liquid swirling inside.

ALEX

But possibilities are a good thing. They give us strength and hope for the future.

SARAH

Not the way he sees it. Take us, for example. The way he sees the world, we weren't meant for one another. It was all a factor of timing, location and coincidence.

ALEX

Right place ...

SARAH
(Nodding)
... Right time.

SARAH stares across the table at ALEX and taps the side of her nose. She turns to BRILL and scrunches her face at him.

SILVANA (V.O.)
Without intending to do so, we'd managed to pull these two into our scene as it was still being written, and neither was the wiser. At first I felt a bit like a fraud or an imposter, like we were tricking these two unsuspecting participants into taking part in something without either one of them knowing what was really going on.
(Beat)
But the conversation dragged on. It became a bit thrilling, watching two complete strangers riff on our incomplete scene. The rush of it quickly overwhelmed whatever hesitation I might have felt. When Sarah gave Brill a teasing sneer, it was hard not to draw a possible future for their relationship. I imagined that sneer in later years turning sour and defiant as time passed and the divide between them -- between her fate and his coincidence -- grew from a crack in the pavement to a collapsed sinkhole in the road outside their second mortgage, to a gaping maw

straight through from one end of the planet to the other.

SARAH

But he's wrong. We were fated to be together. I *know* it.

SARAH turns to BRILL. They both lean in at the same time and KISS each other on the lips.

SILVANA

How can you be so sure?

SARAH

Because the proof that there is a plan is sitting right in front of me. Just look at Alex, Silvana. Look at how he looks at you.

SILVANA'S eyes flit over to ALEX, who smiles a mix of shyness and seduction. He tightens his grip on SILVANA'S hand.

SILVANA (V.O.)

I'd noticed you stealing glances at me all night but said nothing. It was fun, feeling like we were a couple of high schoolers still getting a feel for one another -- away, for a night, from deception, destruction and death.

(Beat)

You'd just come off your largest role to date, a full half an act of screen time selling your way through a primrose-

and-picket-fence stable of stay-at-home wives and soccer moms -- that is, of course, until the husbands and boyfriends of the neighbourhood discovered your garden-treading ways. They dragged you across the pavement by your ankles, locked you in the trunk of a Camaro and pushed it off the edge of a cliff.

(Beat)

You've always had such a knack for bringing people together.

(Beat)

I'd driven into town separately and surprised you after work, as you were on your way back to the hotel the studio had set you up in.

CUT TO:

INT: FREMONT HOTEL & CASINO / ROOM 612 (FLASHBACK) -- NIGHT

SILVANA is sitting on the edge of the bed, waiting. The door to the room opens and ALEX enters, his JACKET slung over his right shoulder. SILVANA stands and walks over to him, taking the JACKET from his hands.

SILVANA

How was your day?

ALEX

Good, honey, real good.

SILVANA

Did ... did anything special happen?

ALEX

No, not really. Just your typical day. But boy howdy, I am beat.

SILVANA hangs the JACKET up in the closet next to the entrance to the bathroom.

SILVANA (V.O.)

You lied so effortlessly. I should have been more concerned about that fact than I was.

(Beat)

Later that night, over dinner, you talked insurance sales figures, gabbed about your goals for the month, said that if you didn't meet your quota there'd be hell to pay -- real fire and brimstone, you said, convincing both of us in the moment.

ALEX and SILVANA sit down on the edge of the bed. ALEX strokes SILVANA'S hair and smiles sweetly. SILVANA returns the smile.

SILVANA (V.O.) (Cont.)

You said nothing at all about your on-paper affairs, each one detailed in the script like notches in a headboard. I could see them, though, in the twinkle in your eye, hidden from your wife who wasn't really your wife because this was just how far you were willing to take things. It didn't matter that I'd read the script and knew your character's flaws.

(Beat)

What bothers me now, looking back on that night together in Vegas, is how readily I forgave you your non-existent transgressions. Like it was something I was supposed to do. Or expected to do. I did it because I was more Silvana then than I realized.

CUT TO:

INT: BELLAGIO RESORT & CASINO / PETROSSIAN BAR -- LATE NIGHT

SARAH, exhaustion and alcohol getting the best of her, puts her head on BRILL'S shoulder and closes her eyes. BRILL leans back in his seat and SIGHS HAPPILY.

SILVANA (V.O.)

They were like a postcard pair on their second honeymoon. I couldn't help but wonder if it had been as happy a seven-year stint as they made it out to be, or if they were, in fact, better actors than even you or I. Soon I began to wonder if that was the case with everyone we met as a pair -- if the individuals and couples who crossed our paths were who they said they were, or if they, too, were living under assumed identities, assumed vocations, mirrors of our own distorted ambition.

CUT TO:

INT: BELLAGIO RESORT & CASINO / LOBBY -- LATE NIGHT

Some time after saying their farewells to SARAH and BRILL, ALEX and SILVANA are wandering the resort's lobby, hand in hand, casually admiring the architecture and opulence. They stop beneath the *FIORO DI COMO* -- a sculpture comprised of more than two thousand blown glass flowers adorning the ceiling of the resort's lobby.

M_____ (V.O.)

We died without ever saying our goodbyes to the walk-on friends we met and pulled -- without their knowledge or consent -- into our tiny, transient worlds. We were living the modern myth of Bill Murray -- popping up out of nowhere, inserting ourselves into the lives of others, giving them a taste of our fiction and disappearing again just as mysteriously. The difference being, no one actually knew or cared who we were. Once you'd gotten tired of the writing or the backdrop of a place, we shelved our skins of different types and moved on to whatever was next for you. You continued to leave notes and script pages for me -- ellipses, bread crumbs guiding our way from one life to the next. They were clues as to your next performance and our next pair of lives. Though we never discussed it, I felt the gradual disappearance of our masturbatory pretense -- gone was the illusion that I was a different person in bed with you each night. Whatever the exterior, I started to feel like we were on the same emotional wavelength, you and I. Our paths to this point had differed, but an understanding had silently been reached.

ALEX, still holding SILVANA's hand, playfully swings her arm in the air.

M_____

(Staring at the ceiling)

It's beautiful.

ALEX

It's something all right.

M_____ (V.O.)

I sighed louder than intended -- I could still hear it in your voice, the slight Southern charm you'd used to win the affections of an entire neighbourhood's worth of women. You were still Alex, but I didn't want to be Silvana any longer. I wanted to stare up at that stunning one-of-a-kind ceiling as myself, to keep its memory for myself.

M_____

I like it here. It feels right.

ALEX

(Slightly frustrated)

We can always come back, once I've hit my quota for the month.

M_____

D____, I --

ALEX SQUEEZES SILVANA's HAND. She WINCES in pain.

ALEX

We'll come back. I promise.

SILVANA

(Reluctantly)

... When?

ALEX

Someday.

SILVANA

Do you promise?

ALEX

On my life.

SILVANA

Which one?

24. The Sum of One's Life

Posted: 03/29/2014

It's distressing to think that in the early days of the studio system, MGM kept such intimate tabs on their celebrities that they even had a chart tracking the menstrual cycles of all their actresses. Think about that for a second, about that level of control, about how ready they were to create new histories and biographies for all their actors and actresses – about how many changed their names, their very identities, to better market themselves. Marilyn Monroe was born Norma Jeane Mortenson, Doris Day was Doris Mary Ann Kappelhoff, Greta Garbo, Greta Lovisa Gustafsson ... The lesson of the day: never underestimate the power of effective alliteration.

Celebrity couplings have also been scrutinized and picked at and portmanteau'd as much as any other facet of the industry – from Brangelina and the two separate comings of Bennifer all the way back to Mary Pickford and Douglas Fairbanks, whose Hollywood mansion was, of course, called Pickfair. It was this side of the industry – the public's adoption and unmitigated worship of celebrity culture – that D_____ equally hated and feared. He loved making movies, sure, and being a part of the big machine, but he never wanted the spotlight for himself. Maybe someone would even think him a role model – that would be a hell of a different sort. No, we were never so famous that this was a concern. He was a death scene artist through and through, and I was ...

Well, nobody special, I fucking suppose.

It does make one wonder, though, how the unwitting players and found friends we accumulated over the short time of our relationship would react upon reading these entries – seeing their memories of us pulled into a new and altogether unflattering light as part of a larger, still mostly unwritten story. I hope some of them are reading this, I really do; in my weaker moments I feel a certain amount of guilt for what we concealed – the falsehoods we presented to everyone we came in contact with, from Sarah and Brill and others like them, to those whose flesh and memories we regularly plundered – and I find myself wondering where they are and what they're doing. For them, and for so many, this conversation must be frustratingly one-sided; we're all waiting to hear from D_____, wherever he is, whatever he's doing. If he's still reading. If he was ever reading this at all, or if it was merely Ezra acting on his behalf. If any part of him feels anything at all about the shadow narrative I've pieced together.

I'm sorry. It's easy these days to tumble down a rabbit hole of what-ifs: What if I'd never left home in the first place? What if I'd kept my foot out of Hollywood and stuck to the obits? What if we'd never sat next to one another at craft services? What if I'd never gone to meet him that night at the Galaxy?

When I start down one of these trains of thought, my mind goes to Louise, who used to tell me the world was too short to wonder *what if* – that there'd be more than enough people who doubted you throughout your life, hitchhikers along your path with nowhere to go and nothing better to do than to make you feel like shit. That you shouldn't give those people the time of day. "Don't let the bastards win," she said once when I was still in high school, while helping me adjust a face mask in the mirror – Tess Chisholm from down the street. Louise had noticed Tess one day, rollerblading by while we were on our way home from Skyline Market with two giant bags of sour keys – something we used to do all the time when we were kids, and still did every time she returned home for a visit or to do a load of laundry. "She's cute," she said. "She'd look real nice on you."

Aud voiced something similar once. It was one of the rare instances where she dropped all pretense and was, best I could tell, her naked self. I'd just been dumped by another on-set coffee runner who thought they could do better than to date an extra, who chided me for my lack of attention to detail – who, one night, picked at the half-sleeve I wore over just my legs, to give my profile something more than just a straight edge, and said, "Is this the best you can do?"

"Dumb fucking fuckboys," she said while wrapping her hair up in a towel. We were in the bathroom in her apartment on Sunset and she'd just gotten out of the shower. I sat on the toilet seat, half watching her, half staring at the space between my feet. "They don't know a good thing when they have it, ya?"

"What if he's right, though? What if I need to be trying harder? What if I'm not enough?"

And she knelt in front of me, her hair and body wrapped in towels so soft I shuddered at their imagined cost, and said, "I'm going to tell you this, M______, and I'm going to tell you this once: You are enough. You're more than enough. You're the light of my life – and don't you ever fucking forget it."

And I started to cry and was about to thank her when she turned back to the mirror and started admiring herself in profile. "Fuck, I need to get back to the gym. Am I looking soft to you?"

I stared at her then, tears in my eyes. "You're perfect," I said, and I wasn't even thinking about her skin.

You were perfect, Aud. And you still are.

The two of them, Aud and Louise both, they wanted me to know that I was strong, stronger than I believed myself to be. With D_____, though, it was different. That night, two Septembers ago, when he corrected me in the Bellagio's lobby for using his real name, I felt weakened, hollowed out. It was like he'd taken away my strength. *I* thought that ceiling was beautiful and *I* wanted to tell him about it. I didn't know what Silvana thought about it and I didn't care either. I still don't. It was the moment that mattered. It was a small moment, but those are what make us *us*. I wish, right there, in the middle of one of the most watched hotels in the world, that I'd had enough sense of self to claw my way out of Silvana's sleeve, to leave D_____ on his own, holding the limp hand of eight or nine different strangers that had been so worthlessly pieced together.

††

Whenever I designed a new sleeve, I pulled from what I knew. Sometimes it was friends and family that served as my inspiration; other times there was more than enough detail written into the script I'd been provided, and all I had to do was find the right patterns and tones to piece it all together. My early attempts were spotty at best, riddled with holes in the designs and loose stitches that if pulled would cause an entire sleeve to unravel like slabs of meat through a deli slicer – to fall apart, to fall away from me. Those initial sleeves were like the characters in a child's choose-your-own-adventure novel, constructed from branching dialogue trees and abstract, out-of-left-field outcomes. But the core of each design was still me: my thoughts, my feelings, my desires. When D_____ tried to subvert that, to depress even the smallest pieces of me ...

For a time – longer than was healthy – I tried doing something different: outlining and designing new potential sleeves for both of us, from scratch, with few or no ties to who we really were on the outside. It was instantly more difficult than I'd imagined it would be; the background minutia required was staggering and I was quickly overwhelmed by all the ways it could go wrong, all the ways it might shatter the illusion if not done with enough consideration. Do you have any idea as to the level of detail required to make a fictitious character seem real? Let's pull a scenario out of the closet, strictly for shits and giggles.

We start with the basics: genre. How about science fiction – we've not done that in a while. All right now, let's say we do one for D_____, for the type of leading role that twenty or twenty-five years ago might have kicked his career into a different stratosphere: a boy living in a piss-poor part of town tasked with fighting off an alien invasion.

So what's first? Appearance, naturally: basic physical structure. We could pull an archetype out of a hat, but that would be a waste of time, and besides, we're better than that. Let the details forge the flesh, right? Motivation: he's tough, though not as tough as he thinks, and he feels like he needs to prove himself at all times, which he'll get to do by defending his home. Why? It's all he's got. Survey says: rags; riches alienate younger viewers. An impoverished life is a relatable life – that's character building 101. Besides, there aren't enough one-percenters in the world to carry a box office. Now, why's our boy so railroad-spike tough? Because of his friends, and because of the part of the city he's from – inner city, slumburbia. How's he going to react to the extreme circumstances of an alien invasion? Why he's going to be cool, calm and collected, of course, *because* he's inner city, *because* death and drug abuse and all those scary things are practically nothing to him. So aliens? Fuck aliens – vagina-lipped hunchbacks don't stand a web-footed chance in hell. For both our protagonist and his friends, the slums are all they got, so this collection of stray dogs is going to fight to protect their lot 'til the bitter climax.

Next up, background: Why is our hero poor? His mother's dead and his father's an absentee junkie who comes home once a week to crash on the sofa and smack his kid around. He puts the "fun" in the "fundamentals of proper parenting." So who's our hero living with when he's not out defending the projects with his very life or busy being a broken beer bottle's pincushion? Aunt or uncle: aunt means we give him another layer, a dormant one that occasionally rises to the surface when he needs to show just how caring and conscientious he can be when not so concerned with keeping up his tough motherfucker exterior; uncle, on the other hand, hardens him further, and our boy is sent out in the first act, prior to the alien's invasion, to pick his uncle's womanizing ass up some booze and smokes. Then, finally, we get back to the specifics: height, weight, race and age, all multi-faceted details in their own right. Each decision contains multitudes of their own for consideration: How will the audience react to a Black protagonist versus a White one? A man instead of a woman? A young adult in place of a teenager? A straight character versus a queer one? Each one of these, along with a few hundred more micro-decisions, will affect and potentially change all previously mentioned possibilities.

To summarize: D_____ never respected just how hard I worked to make our fiction feel real.

††

I did something a couple of days ago that I hadn't done since high school, back when I first started messing around with obit writing: I crashed someone's funeral. It wasn't exactly planned; I needed to get away from this blog and do some thinking, so I went out for a long walk (and a short bus ride) and wound up passing Evergreen Memorial. A fair distance from the cemetery's entrance I saw a large group of people – so many that from where I stood they looked like a swarm of blackflies all hovering around the same piece of meat. My first response was to keep moving, but there was something to seeing so many people hugging one another, holding one another ... I couldn't help myself – I wanted to know what sort of person could've elicited such a dramatic response from so many at once. I crossed the cemetery's threshold and made my way as unassumingly as possible to the perimeter of the swarm.

The closer I got to the group, the more I heard ... not sniffling, not even really crying, but ... laughter. Not loud, but still, identifiable chuckles could be heard. As I circled the group, I caught several snippets of dialogue: "Do you remember the time she ..." "Oh God, I can't believe we didn't wind up in jail ..." "Never met someone so giving ..."

"You're not supposed to be here," said a receding voice. I turned around and saw, ten feet away, a young woman of twenty or so leaning against a headstone, her palms gripping the top of the weathered rock. She was dressed in a form-fitting black dress with long dyed-black hair that covered her eyes and fell down the front of her chest.

I walked toward her. "I'm sorry, what did you say?"

"You're not supposed to be here," she said again. "This isn't your family."

"No," I said, "it's not."

"Then what are you doing here?"

I could have lied – I could have walked her away from the group, cracked her head on a concrete cross, picked up a jagged branch or piece of stone and split open and slipped into her skin before any of her grieving family members even knew she was gone. She had the type of porcelain skin that would show a single stitch; if I wanted to hide inside her, she'd have to be taken whole.

I could've finished my work and slid inside her skin, and then gone back to the rest of them thirty minutes, maybe an hour later, and acted the part of their daughter or niece or cousin or grandchild, and not one of them would have been the wiser.

"I'm here," I said, choosing the truth less taken, "because I was walking by the cemetery and I saw a lot of love on display. And I wanted to know about the sort of person who could pull so many people together in one spot."

"It's a funeral," she said, glibly. "People crawl out of the woodwork for shows like these."

"Not like this," I said, staring back at the rather impressive gathering.

"Been to a lot of funerals, have you?"

"I've seen my share."

The girl squinted at me as if deciding whether or not I was telling the truth – or worth telling the truth to. "She was my great-grandmother," she said at last. "She was one hundred and seven when she died."

Just think about that number: one hundred and seven. It's a digit few of us can ever hope to reach. I suppose, all things being equal, the better question would be whether or not we *deserve* to live that long.

Instead of saying something comforting or introspective, I whistled and said, "Wow."

"Yeah ... wow." Her disinterest in me was palpable.

"I didn't mean ... It's just impressive, that's all."

"I guess. Gran-Gran met a lot of people in her time. She made a lot of friends." The young woman in black proceeded to tell me about her great-grandmother – Sheilagh Watson – and how she lived her life, how she built the family and legacy that surrounded her grave, huddled arm in arm, sharing memories of their time with the deceased. As it was, Sheilagh had led a life of some notoriety. She'd been a flirt, she'd even done some time – for grand theft auto, no less, when she was just a teenager – but she'd had fun, and she'd always been as open about the skeletons in her closet as she'd been about the love she had for her husband of sixty-three years and their seven daughters, all matriarchs in their own right. From an early age Sheilagh taught her daughters the two most important things she knew: to be yourself and to lead a life of inclusion, not exclusion – to make sure that when they write the summary of your life's experiences, every individual chapter is the size of a goddamn book. Do those two things and you will die without an ounce of regret, without thinking, "if only I did this," or "if only I'd done that."

As it is, life is a game of final sums – of years lived, lives touched, dreams pursued and goals met, the net result of which can be seen by counting the bowed heads at one's funeral. Sheilagh's final sum was 112. That's how many people showed up that day at Evergreen Memorial. It's a legacy by which even the biggest stars would feel honoured, if only their histories were as genuine.

D_____ called me transient once. I rejected it; the very notion of it was detestable. But now I see it, his terrible, prophetic tendencies at work. My own final sum is fast approaching and the math isn't pretty.

"You look like hell," the young woman in black said after she'd finished telling me about her great-grandmother's life.

"What?"

She pointed a narrow, ghostly finger at my face. "Your skin, it's all gross and chalky. Like it's ready to come away from your bones. You should probably see a doctor about that."

"Yeah." I reached up and put two fingers to the side of my face, rubbing the sleeveless skin, feeling like I could puncture my brittle cheek with very little force. The honesty of my appearance was revolting. "I probably should."

25. Bonnie and Clyde Redux

Posted: 04/05/2014

INT: RIDE 'EM HARD BAR AND GRILL -- NIGHT

PATRICK (29-year-old White male) and his pregnant bride SHARON (27-year-old Black female) sit across a picnic bench-style table from CLAUD (44-year-old White male) and BONITA (30-year-old Latino female). There are three beers on the table, and a glass of water in front of SHARON.

PATRICK stares at CLAUD, dumbfounded, while SHARON and BONITA look on in surprise.

SHARON

(Disbelief)

Come again?

CLAUD grins charismatically.

CLAUD

We rob banks.

SHARON

You ... you rob banks.

CLAUD nods.

CLAUD

Yes, Ma'am.

CLAUD wraps his arm around BONITA'S waist, affectionately pinches the skin of the sleeve.

CLAUD (Cont.)

Just the two of us. We've been doing it for going on seven years now.

SHARON

I ... I don't even know what to ...

(Beat)

How many have you robbed?

CLAUD turns and looks at BONITA.

CLAUD

What is it now, sweetheart, thirty, give or take?

BONITA

(Quietly)

Give or take.

BONITA (V.O.)

I said, in my best English-as-a-

second-language stutter.

(Beat)

Sharon was genuinely taken aback by what you'd said. Or maybe just taken in -- the two wide-eyed stares are often indistinguishable from one another.

SHARON

Isn't that dangerous? In this day and age, aren't you more likely to be caught or killed than anything else?

CLAUD shrugs nonchalantly.

CLAUD

We need the money. We don't harm anyone, and the government will cover the bank's ass. It's totally victimless. Easy in, easy out.

BONITA (V.O.)

I almost felt bad for Patrick and Sharon. It was five days from Halloween and we were down near the Mexican border where you'd been working as a former bank robber turned drug runner crossing the border with a busload of tourists and an assload of tightly wrapped plastic baggies of joy and happiness at seven-fifty a gram. You'd wrapped earlier that afternoon, gunned down sprinting from the border police while the two men you'd been travelling with remained on the ground, their knees in the sand with their hands locked, fingers interlaced behind their heads, and rifles pressed up against their spines. You'd been given fair warning but you didn't listen.

(Beat)

They shot you twice -- first in your leg, and then, when that barely slowed you down, they fired again. The bullet went straight through your heart, and you tumbled to the ground, came down hard on your left side, and bled out into the dirt and dust of the New Mexican desert.

(Beat)

We decided to celebrate that night at a dive you'd spotted fifty miles from the middle of nowhere. Patrick and Sharon were there on their first night as husband and wife following a shotgun wedding. When you saw them cuddling up to one another, Patrick's hand on his new wife's blossoming stomach, you smiled at me, devilishly, signalling you were ready to play. Eyes on them as they danced, you waited for just the right moment, between kisses that looked like one drunken mother bird feeding another, and swept in, taking her by the arms. Both were so inebriated with joy that neither felt offended. Patrick fun-punched you in the arm, warning you to stay away from his bride of precisely six hours and twenty-five minutes. With that happy pronouncement, you offered to buy a round for the group and we migrated to a table, where, when prodded by Patrick, investment portfolio guru for one of the nation's three largest banks, as to what you did for a living, you immediately revealed your scripted and very illegal past.

PATRICK leans forward, elbows on the table, cradling the beer in front of him with both hands.

PATRICK

(Disbelief)

So ... you're saying you rob banks. Like, really rob them.

CLAUD

And we do it with style.

SHARON

You're pulling our legs.

CLAUD sips from his beer and puts it down again.

CLAUD

Nothin' doin', ma'am.

PATRICK pushes his beer to the centre of the table.

PATRICK
This is horseshit. You're just some clown trying to get a rise out of us.

CLAUD'S smile grows.

BONITA takes a drink.

BONITA (V.O.)
I thought maybe I should say something, but then I saw your smile -- full Cheshire cat -- and realized I didn't know my cues. So I held back and waited to see where you were taking us.

CLAUD
My friend, no horse has ever shit so sweet. But I am enjoying how much this is getting to you, if the truth must be told.

SHARON leans forward with her elbows on the table and her head resting in her palms.

SHARON
(Fascinated)
Why take such a risk?
(Beat)
Aren't you the least bit afraid of what might happen?

CLAUD
Whatever happens happens, and there ain't one thing we can do 'bout it.

BONITA (V.O.)

The cockier you got, the more you let your Southern swagger fly. For a moment I feared you were about to lose control and go full-blown Dukes of Hazzard *on our poor, unsuspecting company.*

CLAUD

There's simply too much fun to be had for us to hang up our spurs and walk away.

PATRICK slides out of his seat and stands up. He holds his hand out for SHARON.

PATRICK

(Angrily)

Come on. We need to get out of here.

SHARON

In a minute -- I want to hear more.

PATRICK

No.

PATRICK grabs SHARON'S hand and starts to pull her out of her seat. She resists.

PATRICK

We can't be listening to this. If anyone from my work were to find out ... We can't risk getting implicated in ... whatever this is. We have to go and we have to go now.

CLAUD stands up and moves between PATRICK and SHARON, his arms up, palms out peacefully.

CLAUD

Now wait just a minute here. If the lady wants to stay, you've got no right to --

PATRICK

(Furious)

I've got every damn right in the world and then some. Come on, Sharon. Let's get out of here. Now.

PATRICK pushes CLAUD out of the way. He tugs harder on SHARON'S hand. She WINCES uncomfortably.

SHARON

Pat, stop it, you're hurting me.

CLAUD steps between them again.

CLAUD

Hold up, now just think about this for a --

PATRICK releases SHARON'S hand. He makes a FIST and PUNCHES CLAUD in the face.

CLAUD falls to the ground.

CUT TO BLACK

26. Bonnie and Clyde Redux, Part II

Posted: 04/05/2014

Thirty minutes later we were in a rental car, driving back to LA together for the first time as just us. Actually I should say that I was doing all the driving, as you were busy holding a rapidly melting Ziploc bag full of ice to your right eye. Mile by silent mile you just stared out the passenger window, into the dark.

"So what was all that about?" I asked when the prolonged absence of dialogue had gotten too uncomfortable, like the screenwriter in your head had been struck with sudden writer's block. "You feel like filling me in? Since when did you start getting off putting a torch to people's feet?"

And still you said nothing, preferring to pout over your bruised and battered ego.

"Not now," I said. I cleared my throat of Bonita's voice. When I spoke, I felt the flesh of her lips rattling against my own, flapping loose. A tremor separated her skin from mine as I continued to drive. "If you want to keep looking blindly away, do it on your own time. You almost got us into a helluva mess back there and I want to know why – I *deserve* to know why. Talk to me. *You*-you – Galaxy Drive-In–you."

That's when I heard it – a low moan, barely audible over the sound of the car's engine.

"What was that?"

"Don't do this," you said – *you* said. "Don't ruin things for us."

"I just want to know what's going on, you know. Inside. I want ... I need you to give me something to go on. It doesn't have to be anything huge. Just ... more than this silent treatment crap. I've earned that much."

Still you said nothing. I looked over at you and saw, in the subtle glare of the moon, that your face had begun to swell like an overripe fruit. The back of my hand started to itch, so I reached over and massaged the sleeve, scratched, bore a hole right through to the underflesh. The night air was cool on my real skin, soothing, and I wanted to pull over and strip – just rip it all off, completely discard Bonita, leave her by the side of the road.

It wouldn't matter, though. You wouldn't have listened any more to me than you would have Bonita. And if you or anyone else were to ask me now, I still don't know if I could tell you what compelled me to do what I did next.

"*... you know, when we started out, I thought we was really goin' somewhere ... but this is it – we're just goin', huh?*"

"No," you said, sharply. You caught on immediately. "Don't do that."

"*Not as long as you care about me*," I said in my very best Faye Dunaway, ignoring the line of dialogue I knew you'd missed because I'd watched the film once a fucking week since Richard Thorn slipped between my sheets and into my life.

"This isn't yours to fuck around with. Stop it – stop it now."

"*Enough to die with me, baby? 'Cause I think that's where we're goin' ... I surely do –*"

"Stop it!" you said, and reached for the steering wheel. "Not fucking now – don't do this now!" *Why*, I wondered. *Because they were yours? Because you weren't ready to share them after all? Or was it because you'd just been knocked down by someone who didn't give two shits about our script?* I pushed your hands away and you hit me in the shoulder, pressed me up against the driver's side window until I cried for you to stop. I swerved off the side of the road and we careened down a small embankment. I pumped the brakes.

We crashed to a halt, and you unbuckled your seat belt and reached over, grabbing my chest, squeezing, twisting the skin between your fists into two pale, gnarled roses. I could feel the sleeve stretching beyond its limits, small holes appearing in the surface as cold air slipped into the space between Bonita's skin and my own, and you stared and you huffed and you let go and snarled at me to get us the fuck back on the road.

We drove the rest of the way in wounded, brittle silence. Only occasionally I glanced over at you, but you never once looked back. You froze me out, like you're still doing to this day. It doesn't matter though. It's done. It happened. And we're getting to the real meat of things now. We're getting to the very heart of you.

You know what you done there? you would've said if you were half the "him" you wanted to be. *You told my story, you told my whole story right there, right there. One time I told you I was gonna make you somebody. That's what you done for me. You made me somebody they're gonna remember.*

I'm trying. I'm really trying here.

Clyde Barrow you ain't, and you fucking never will be.

27. That Time You Killed Me and I Didn't Die

Posted: 04/12/2014

I received a letter in the mail yesterday, with no return postage, no signature, just a single paragraph of text written in neat, precise block letters like those used by a primary schoolteacher when teaching the alphabet for very the first time. The words begged me to stop, pleading for leniency, citing a career on the line. Saying, in closing, *Please, listen to your conscience. Do the right thing.*

And just when we're getting to the best part, too.

Immediately, I pictured D_____ writing this letter, using the back of a hardcover book, or a prop, or a copy of his latest script as a makeshift desk, delicately crafting each letter so as to remove all traces of self while some special effects grunt he's probably worked with more than a dozen times already but would never care enough to recognize straps a blood packet to his chest, so that when the jilted ex-lover catches him in bed with her best friend and fires a single bullet through the bedsheet, he'll bleed a thick line drawing through the white like a felt pen snapped in half. And then I woke up and realized what a fool I was.

Listen to my conscience ... Ezra. Just stop. Please. This has gotten embarrassing. I've still got plenty of story left to tell and I don't know how much time I have left in which to do it, and I will not allow you to get in my way. Not for anything in the world.

††

That night, D_____, I hesitated when you slumped back in the passenger seat and told me – ordered me – to get us back on the road. I looked down at my chest then, at the two fistfuls of skin you'd savagely grabbed hold of and how they'd retained the twisted shape you'd formed. The stitching around where the skin of the left breast met the *V* of my neck had split open, sending a chill between the sleeve and the body housed within. I no longer wished to strip myself clean of Bonita; I felt too naked as it were, too exposed. Instead, I thought of driving to the nearest town, finding someone – anyone – whose pattern might fit, taking from them, repairing myself and retreating further into the sleeve already on.

I drove on the side of the road for a bit, until the ground levelled out again and I was able to get us back on the highway. Like I said, the rest of the way back to LA we travelled in complete silence; it was like being alone in the car. Three hours later, tired and just ... just done with it all, I pulled up in front of a building you'd never seen before.

"Where are we?" you said. The words scraped out of you like sandpaper.

"Home. This is where I live. Second floor, suite –"

You jumped out of the car and slammed the door before I could finish. I climbed quickly from the driver's seat and watched as you stalked off down the street. I shouted at you, said something like, "You can't keep running from me!" but you never stopped, never turned back.

††

It was three weeks later, in mid-November, at the start of the zombie apocalypse, when I saw D_____ for the very last time.

He called – for the first time ever he actually used a phone and called me. I wasn't aware he even knew my number; I figured he must have gotten it from some studio file, or maybe Ezra dug it up for him – against her better recommendation, I'm certain. His voice was panic-stricken. He said he needed to see me, that he needed to make things right before –

And then the line went dead.

My first thought: it was some low-rent thriller, and he was part of the first act's body count. In my mind I saw him dropping the phone and taking off running, seeking help or shelter or a way out – any way out – from whatever disaster movie cliché he'd found himself in the middle of. As if it were a reflex, I instantly started piecing together an image of a strife- or battle-worn sleeve, a body that had seen more than its share of horrors yet still managed to carry on. He'd come rushing through my door and throw his tired body into my arms, and I'd tell him that he was safe there, with me, that we could deal with whatever was happening out there so long as we dealt with it together.

No, I thought. *Not again. Not fucking again.* I swore to myself when he walked away from the car after the trip home from New Mexico that I was done letting him drag me into whatever personalized hell was next on his list. It was finished – I wanted to burn every single sleeve hanging limp and vacant in my closet, everything that was linked to him in any way. I wanted the smoke from their flesh, the waxy, awful stench, to clog my airway and suffocate me beneath the miserable realization of all that I'd left behind.

††

You called again an hour later. Your voice was hoarse, and you were huffing into the receiver as if you'd just come in from a run. I couldn't tell at that point who you were even trying to be.

D____
(Exhausted)
I'm safe. For now, anyway.

"Look," I said while pacing my apartment, staring for a moment at the mirror on the dresser in front of me – at the two softball-sized purple blotches on my chest that had not even started to fade. "I ... I don't think I can do this anymore. I think ... I'm tired, D____. Of this. Of us."

D____
Listen to me! I'm not fucking around right now. Shit's gone out of control and I need a place to lay low for a while.

"No. Don't even think about it. Out of bounds."

D____
You've got to help me!

"Not this time. Not until you drop this."

D____
I can't go back out there. Not after everything that's happened. Not after ... all those bodies ... they were everywhere, strewn all over the place ... broken, torn in two, and ... and ...

"I'm hanging up," I said.

D____
I'm coming over.

"No, you're not."

D____

I'll be there as soon as possible. Keep a light burning for me. I'll outrun this hoard if it's the last thing I --

"Shut up and listen to me, *please*. You are *not* coming over here."

D____

Wish me luck.

"Fuck you with a fence post."

D____

I'll see you soon, love.

And the line went dead again.

It was only ten, maybe fifteen minutes later that he was pounding on my door, begging me to let him in, screaming his throat raw. Because, of course, his life was at risk from zombie hoards or biker gangs or rabid Shriners or whatever the fuck. *Don't do it*, I said to myself. *Don't let him in.*

D____

(Frantic)

Don't do this to me! They're coming for me, and they're going to kill me if they find out where I am!

Furious, borderline apoplectic, I opened the door and pulled him inside before any of my neighbours felt an urge to call the police and report the very unhinged idiot screaming bloody murder through the hallway.

Do you have any idea what he looked like right then? Like a junkie, strung out on meth, ready to chew a hole through his bottom lip. He stunk, too, like ground beef and motor oil. If he'd revealed to me that he'd been squatting for the better part of a week in the Dumpster behind a McDonald's I'd have believed it.

Before the door had even closed he'd locked his arms around my neck and was thanking me, reciting his love for me as if I'd actually just saved his sorry skin. And his voice – it was more his than I was used to hearing by this point. I pushed him away – the stench of rotting meat was too sickening to ignore.

"What is this?" I said. "You're method acting as a homeless man now?"

```
                    D____

          (Hurt)
     I don't ... What are you talking
     about?
```

"You reek. You smell like you've been rolling in pig shit."

What happened next I remember vividly; the scene is etched into my brain. He smiled at me, as if he was expecting a punchline to follow my previous statement. Once he realized none was coming, however, his smile turned sour and D_____ parted his teeth with his tongue.

```
                    D____

          (Angry)
     So terribly sorry to have bothered you.
     I'd hate to think my literal peril was
     an inconvenience or anything. I'll
     just go and toss myself into the mouth
     of hell then.
```

"Oh, fuck right off with that. There's no murderous hoard out for your blood. Listen to me very carefully now: nothing and no one is hunting you. You're alone and you stink like a vegan on a bean kick."

He nodded several times, but said nothing. If he was actually hurt or just playing I couldn't tell. Then, like he'd suddenly remembered why he'd come in the first place, he stepped forward and pulled a scrunched up collection of papers from his back pocket. D_____ thrust them at me; they were damp with sweat.

"What's this?" I asked.

He twitched, the pages shaking in his hand.

"No. No way," I said, backing away from the loose pages of script. I could see fresh ink written over some of the type – dialogue, I imagine, for whoever he dreamed me to be. "I'm done. I'm finished with all that."

D_____

Take it.

I shook my head. "No."

"*Take it!*" he shouted.

I heard movement in the room adjacent, quiet shuffling along the floor as if they were wearing plastic bags on their feet, like at a crime scene. In my head I pictured my neighbours huddled against the thin wall separating our apartments with a single drinking glass shared between them, pressed up against the surface as they listened to every soap-operatic invective. I snatched the pages from his outstretched hand and looked at them before he could scream again. Scenes from a plague flick: somewhere, somehow, a diseased monkey that escaped from a classified pharmaceutical lab had come into contact with a herd of cows, and the resulting illness, a plague the likes of which humanity had not seen since the fourteenth century, swept quickly through the populace leaving most dead, and a few unlucky enough to have risen again as zombies – sorry, I mean, "Plague Z carriers." For fuck's sake, people, a zombie's a zombie no matter what stupid name you give it.

D_____'s character was naive enough to think it was possible to escape something like that. And I, as he'd written me into the margins with his halfway-legible scrawl, was apparently dumb enough to follow him into oblivion. I quickly scanned through the pages while he paced in front of me like an agitated Jack Russell terrier. We were nameless lovers; he was coming for me, to see if I was okay, to hide out from the dead and dying, futilely assuming there was some place to go or something we could do to stave off the coming end of humanity. As he'd written it, I was supposed to welcome him in only to be forced to watch as he sweated through his clothes, the illness taking hold, sapping his remaining strength with incredible speed. Then he died – or was supposed to die – in my arms, the scene ending on an ambiguous note as I coughed softly into my fist, wondering to myself if he'd rise again as one of the infected. Fuck.

Knowing there was no other way to satisfy him, I began to read.

M_____

(Hesitantly)

I ... I was worried about you. I didn't know where you'd gone.

D_____

It's bad out there.

D_____ coughs loudly into his palm. He pulls his hand away and sees BLOOD.

D_____ (Cont.)

Something's happened. Something's going down, something real wrong.

M_____

(Sighs)

What is it?

D____

It's the people, man. It's like they're being turned inside out ... like peeled fruit, insides spilling out all over the place. This is end of days shit.

M_____

Calm down. Tell me what happened.

D____ clutches his sides and doubles over as if kicked in the ribs.

D____

It's a virus, and it's gonna kill us all.

(Hysterical)

Oh god, I don't wanna die!

M_____ gently strokes the side of D____'s face. He is hot to the touch.

M_____

(Lying)

Shhh, it's going to be all right.

D____ shakes his head. His brow is wet and shining with sweat.

D____

No, it ain't.

M_____

Just lie down for a bit. We'll figure this out. I promise.

D____

No ...

M_____

Trust me.

D____

I ...

D____ collapses into M_____'s arms.

M_____ turns D____ over and stares longingly into his eyes, watching as they slowly roll back into his head. D____ GURGLES and GASPS a thick slug's trail of saliva down the side of one cheek.

M_____ holds D____'s body close and begins to cry.

FADE TO BLACK

††

"M_____, are you awake?"

It took a second to register what you'd said – the surprise in hearing my name, my real name, from you. I opened my eyes and saw only darkness, though I could feel you behind me; your back was pressed against mine beneath the sheets, our cold feet touching. For a curious few moments I wondered what was different, why I was so much colder with you than I'd ever been. It was then I realized I was naked – sleeveless – and it was, in fact, the first time our true skins had actually, completely, touched.

I didn't respond to you at first, waiting instead to see if you'd say anything more.

"I've been thinking," you went on. "About Ezra. Is she ... Do you think she's taking advantage of me?"

My voice was barely above a whisper: "What do you mean?"

"I heard her." I could feel you shifting uncomfortably, skating your feet across the mattress as if looking for a warm spot that wasn't there. "Last week, when I went to her office to renew my contract. She doesn't know ... I was outside, waiting for her, and I could hear her talking to someone on the phone."

"What was she saying?" I asked, unsure how long this precarious sincerity would last.

"I thought she was talking about a job for me, but then she started to laugh."

"At what?"

"Me." You paused to collect your thoughts. "She called me her own personal Jesus Christ. She said I just didn't know when to stay dead."

"It was just industry small talk," I said reassuringly, though I didn't for a second believe it. "You can't even be sure she was talking about you."

"Am I a joke?"

I rolled my head toward you, but you were still facing the other direction, looking out my small, barred bedroom window at a street light on the sidewalk outside my building. At the back of your head I saw the beginnings of a bald spot you probably hadn't known was there. A sign that time wasn't standing quite as still as you thought. Proof that you were, in fact, as mortal as every corpse you've portrayed. "You're not a joke," I said.

"How can you know for sure? You don't know anything about me."

I bristled, not knowing if you'd meant it as an admission or an accusation. *Not for lack of trying*, I remember thinking bitterly. Burying the urge to confront you for what you'd just said, I instead lunged at the opportunity. "I want to. I want to know everything there is to know about you."

"It's how she markets me," you continued, abandoning my invitation, leaving it to flicker and die. "I'm the greatest corpse in the business."

"But I thought ..."

"What?"

Exhale. "I thought that's what you wanted to be."

It was impossible to tell in the silence that followed if what I'd said had stung or not. However grim, I'd long ago begun to question what it was you wanted: to live a thousand different lives, embracing each new and unique experience, or to be wiped clean and reborn anew whenever any one life became too claustrophobic.

"I think ..." you began.

"Yes?"

"... one of these days, I'd like to know what it's like to do something else."

"To live?"

"To not die."

††

It was a much different experience, waking up next to you, still in bed with me – in *my* bed, with the real me. Or as real a me as I knew. I remember optimistically thinking we'd turned a corner. I was elated. *Things are going to be different now*, I said to myself. *We'll figure everything out, take life as it comes.* Like this was now some fucking Hallmark movie of the week and we'd been given our second chance, the opportunity to get things right in time for our happily ever after. For ten minutes I lay there on my side, arms crossed beneath my pillow, watching you sleep soundly with your back to me. To this day I wonder if you were faking it; if you could feel my eyes trained on you, half expecting you to leap out of bed, throw on your clothes and barrel out my front door, but hoping with everything I had for the opposite.

When three-quarters of an hour later you finally stumbled out of bed and into my tiny kitchenette, you looked like the lesser of two ... well, zombies. You bumped into the counter, almost tripped over the small curled-up corner of the rug in the middle of the floor. It was like you were hungover, though on what I didn't know. You put your hand out to brace yourself against the wall, and right then I knew something wasn't right.

"Did you sleep okay?" I asked.

You cricked your neck to one side, attempting to stifle a lion's yawn; your breath was a post-slaughter horror show. "Where am I?"

"Home. My home."

"What?"

"Where I live, D_____."

"What did you just say?"

"This is where I live. D_____." A pause, then: "That is your name, isn't it?" I couldn't resist.

At the sound of your real name, the very tenor of the scene changed. I witnessed as your face slowly screwed itself into a minor key, a glimmer of malice in your eyes.

What is it people complain about the most when they go to the movies? They say they couldn't relate to the characters onscreen – that they tried, they really did, but they just didn't care as much as they needed to, or they didn't believe the performances. "If only things had been more relatable ... more realistic." This – and I mean what I'm about to say from the very bottom of my arrhythmic heart – is bullshit. That uncanny valley of realism will never be crossed. You will *never* experience capital *R* reality onscreen, because reality will always be worse. It will always hurt more, seem more evil, feel more antagonistic. What you witness on the screen cannot reflect what it's like to have your organs and muscles eaten away by metastasized shadows until all that's left is a faint silhouette projected outward, or what it's like when your stomach shrinks and contracts and you feel bile rising in you, soaking your throat in a thick primer coat of fire as the person you thought you loved more than anyone advances on you with a glare more villainous than you'd have thought possible.

"Why did you bring me here?" you demanded. Your nasal voice was a high wire stretched tight between two skyscrapers.

I backed up until I bumped into the edge of the kitchen counter behind me. "I didn't. You came here last night on your own."

"No, I didn't. I didn't, I know I didn't. You did something to me."

"Are you ... You look pale. Are you feeling all right?"

"What did you do to me? What's my role?"

"D_____ ..."

"Where is it?" you snapped, loud enough to have woken the neighbours. "Who am I supposed to be?"

It took me a moment to figure out what you were looking for – the crumpled pages of script on the chair next to the bed, wrapped up in a bundle of loose clothing. "I don't know where it is," I said.

You slammed an open palm against the kitchenette counter. "You're lying," you hissed.

"I'm not."

"You know who we're supposed to be and you're keeping it all to yourself."

"You're absolutely right. I know exactly who we're supposed to be. I'm M______ and you're D_____."

"Don't do that."

"Don't what? Say our names? This is us, you fool."

CHARLIE

Malorie, don't you do this to me.

"M______, my name is M______."

RICHARD

Eleanor, this isn't funny.

"My name is M______."

ALEX

Goddamnit, Silv --

"M______, you asshole! My name is M______!"
And you broke stage direction.
And you swung as hard as you could and –

CUT TO BLACK

††

And when I woke up again there was blood.
More than I would have thought.

28. Remembering

Posted: 04/13/2014

Our Relationship (March–November) was a love story of epic proportions and even grander delusions. We lived a hundred different lives together and took just as many along the way.

And then you went and broke my jaw and I couldn't speak or eat solid food for more than a month.

You are survived by me, un-fucking-fortunately for us both.

Act III

29. On the Move

Posted: 05/15/2014

Things change, D_____. Constancy, it seems, is the enemy of progress.

Today it's Jerry's Famous Deli in sunny Marina del Rey, where I'm picking at a slice of carrot cake the size of my head, figuring that if I drag it out over enough hours, and if I can keep it down, it counts as multiple meals. Tomorrow, maybe next week if I'm feeling up to it, I'll bus with my laptop to another Wi-Fi hotspot in the city, where I'll be able to continue our tale unhindered. Now that I know how involved you are in the telling of it – now that I'm aware of the lengths to which you'll go to keep me from finishing – it's my duty to push on, to go forward and complete with total veracity this sad, sordid story.

Eighteen months ago you broke my jaw in two places and fractured my nose. I woke up after twenty minutes spent lying in a pool of my own blood and bits of tooth and gum, and you were already long gone. That was the last I'd seen of you until almost exactly one year later, when Andreas Rain just happened to drag your sorry ass into the spotlight on national television. And now here we are: a mere three weeks ago, *someone* busted down the door to my apartment while I was out at a walk-in clinic, tore open my closet and took out all the sleeves, dumping them on the bed, slicing, frantically cutting them into small, jagged postcards of skin. *Whoever* it was that broke in, they'd searched desperately for something I'm certain was not found.

No, that's not a baseless accusation I'm making – put down the phone, Ezra, before you pull a fucking muscle; your attack dog attorneys will still be there in the morning. I'm not saying it was you or your client that broke into my apartment while I was out that day, nor am I suggesting it was either one of you who took a bat to the dust-covered desktop in the corner of the room when you couldn't figure out the password – COWARDLYMOTHERFUCKER, all one word – all the while making sure not to leave a single visible fingerprint, which I dusted for using the Home Crime Stoppers kit I picked up at the thrift store down the street for just such an occasion. It's so goddamn stupid, too. I mean you know how a blog works, right? It isn't tied to just one computer – this doesn't stop just because you got all smashy-smashy with my personal effects. Anyway, you – or *whomever* – didn't search through a single drawer in the kitchen, didn't go through the nightstand next to the bed ... for fuck's sake, do either of you know the first thing about how to make a home invasion look impersonal? I swear it's like I'm working with amateurs here. You'd think, D_____, with all the roles you've had, all the people we've ... you'd have picked up some basic breaking-and-entering skills along the way.

But whatever. It totally wasn't you guys. I get that. It was probably just some crazed Internet stalker, right?

Forgive me if I come across a bit pissy about the whole thing. It's my birthday and I think this cake and I are entitled to a bit of self-pity. It's strange, though, to think that I've made it this far; when I went to the hospital last summer, back when I was just mostly broke and not completely broke like I am now, complaining of unusually agonizing migraines, and they found the mass in my brain, they said I had maybe six months to a year at best. As it is, we're coming up on month nine and my body still hasn't quit on me. I weigh what feels like half of what I did when you last saw me, D_____, and I'm tired all the time and haven't really worn a sleeve in a lot of weeks, but I'm still here, still visible to anyone bothering to look. Despite all that, it was still a surprise this morning when I woke up and checked the date. I suppose I hadn't given much thought to seeing another birthday, let alone where I'd be or what I'd be doing when that day at last came around again.

It doesn't take much to wear me out these days; I nap whenever and wherever I can, on buses, in quiet corners of hotel lobbies and all-night restaurants and cafés, carrying a backpack filled with my laptop, a disposable burner phone, a couple of pairs of underwear and socks, a toothbrush, some toothpaste and the last few hundred dollars from my savings account. I could go back home – my lease doesn't run out for another six weeks – but it wouldn't be safe to go there now, not after what happened. Because I don't have the protective cushion you do. I don't have a following.

You didn't even know they existed, did you? Trust me, they're out there, and they're voracious. You're their celluloid Lazarus, a phoenix rising from the ashes over and over again. A helpful commenter on my blog posted a link to a website – www.risefromthegrave.net – documenting every on-camera life you've ever led. The site's iconography is a bit crass – your face Photoshopped to the crucified body of Christ with a ticker counting down the months, weeks, days and hours until your next half-minute of screen time drops into theatres nationwide. And then there are the YouTube video compilations – an entire series of mash-ups of every second you've appeared on film, and every single punchlined death, all synched to Clint-fucking-Mansell's "Lux Aeterna," for maximum bravado. Personally I'd have gone with *The Benny Hill Show* theme, or maybe Raymond Scott's "Powerhouse."

How about it, Jesus 2.0? Have you ever sat down and watched one of these compilations? I can't tell you how strange it is, seeing you die on a continuous loop without proper context:

RONNIE BYRNE, a cop on the beat murdered, shot in the head on his last shift before retirement by the same drug lord who'd killed his wife and daughter three years prior begets ...

MICHAEL WRIGHT, a firefighter with three kids and an elderly, cancer-stricken mother at home, who dies rushing into a burning building to save a woman on the fifth floor, is followed by ...

SCOTT LEWIS; AKA SCOTT SMITH; AKA "THE HUNTER," a secret agent plot set-up device who never got to be with the woman he loved because he had to lie about every part of his life to protect her from the former KGB diehards who shot him in the back of the head and sent his body home in edible cubes, naturally bleeding into the life of ...

CHARLIE ELLINGTON; AKA "CHARLIE THE CHIN," a kiss-of-death mob loyalist who smiled the wrong way at a pretty girl with raspberry freckles on her teeth.

By the twelfth video in the series I began to feel a bit like I was circling a drain. The fatalist in me wants to have confidence in the karmic ramifications of a life consisting solely of death and death scenes, dying again and again and in every conceivable way.

The Buddhists would have a field day with you: I'm little more than a wannabe playing dress-up; you, on the other hand, are a prime psychological specimen just waiting to be couched and studied.

The realist in me, however – the better half of our once-was, the part that is *actually* dying – will tell you what I was too afraid to say that night while lying in bed with you: "Yes, Ezra is absolutely taking advantage of you, and you shouldn't stand for it a moment longer."

"But I need her," you'd have implored as if it really were a matter of life and death. "I can't do this without her."

"You can and you fucking will because you're not her supplicant any longer. You want to know what it's like to survive on camera for more than five minutes? Then you've got to ditch mommy dearest."

That night, when you invited the shrill silhouette of your agent into our bed, it was your moment of clarity. I learned about them from Doctor None-of-Your-Business – what it is when one strikes and how much it can knock you around if you're not prepared for it. When you asked me about Ezra, when you tore down that barrier between your work and all your other lives, I think I expected the next day to wake up beside a new you, both of us completely naked, more exposed than we'd ever been. I excitedly thought that we'd tapped a new vein of our relationship. However, those true moments of progress take time – more than I'd anticipated. Your moment of clarity was just that – a moment. Your first. Most certainly our last.

I could at this time offer you another moment of clarity. I could give out our names, your identity and mine, here and now, on this blog for millions to see. But what would be the point? It's easier this way, keeping my distance, even if the safety it offers is but an illusion.

Another thing I learned from Doctor None-of-Your-Business is how to spot a predator. I don't know the sorts of conversations you have with yourself when there's no one around to see the performance – if, in fact, you've shared any of the same thoughts or questions about us that I've had in the months since it all came crashing down. I'd like to think, on occasion, you're able to see through the walls you've put up, to take a moment and glimpse the world that exists on either side.

Ezra doesn't have any such concerns. Make no mistake, D_____: to her you are a meal ticket. Nothing more. Do you think she's ever marketed you as anything *but* a corpse? Maybe she cared more at the beginning of your career, back when you were still a novice cutting your teeth. But I guarantee whatever negligible iota of concern she once held for you died as soon as you exhibited just how amazing you were, and are, at taking a bullet to the face one minute and dying tenderly in someone's arms the next. This is your first lesson in how a person becomes a commodity: you trust the wrong people – the people with the means, motive and opportunity to keep you *transient* – and hurt the right.

You got all that, Ezra? Come on then. Take your best fucking shot.

30. Recovery

Posted: 05/19/2014

I spent three days in the hospital following that whole ordeal where my face tripped and fell into D_____'s fist. They wired my jaw shut, said it would be a few weeks before I could expect to chew or speak again. I don't remember much of the pain; they'd given me a prescription for Tylenol 3, and for the first two weeks I tossed them back like they were Pez candies. One of the nurses gave me a pen and a pad of paper on my second day, once I was alert enough to know fully where I was and what had transpired. She told me if I needed anything to write it down, then she asked me if there was anyone they could get in touch with, and I tried to stop it, the shitty feelings bubbling up inside of me like acid-tinged anxiety, but I couldn't. I started to weep openly, my body shaking where I couldn't scream.

††

Doctor None-of-Your-Business sat up straight in her chair, framed by the degrees adorning the rear wall of her second-floor office. Outside the window above her desk I saw a string of bright white

Christmas lights hung in a loose arch. She smiled politely. "So, M______, is this your first time speaking with a therapist?"

I shook my head. It had been nearly a month since they fixed up my jaw and took out all the hardware, but still it hurt to talk. "Long time ago," I muttered, speaking mostly in consonants. "When I was in high school. I saw somebody then."

"Really," she said, jotting down the information on the legal pad in her lap. At first I was confused; I'd expected her to know all this already. Until, that is, I remembered the hospital records she'd had access to were under the name on my falsified passport, as was my modest employee insurance, now long since evaporated. I suppose it really doesn't matter at this point, to say all of this – no sense skirting around the obvious. Besides, I've already lost everything anyway. "And why was that?"

"Mom thought I was crazy."

"I see ... Was there any particular –"

"I wrote obituaries for the graduating class at my school and put them in the yearbook."

"Oh."

"Yeah."

"The whole class?"

"Also, I wasn't eating. I was ... I wasn't in a good place. I'm okay now, though."

She nodded, hummed an "mm-hmm" and continued writing. She didn't say anything for what must have been at least a paragraph or two. When she looked up at me again, some of the cheer had vanished from her face, replaced by a studious, semi-serious frown. She cleared her throat before speaking again. "Now, can you tell me why you're here today?"

"Because I had my jaw smashed up and didn't really feel like talking to any of my doctors about it," I said frankly. "One of the nurses at the hospital gave me your number in case I decided I had something I wanted to say."

"And do you?" she asked.

"Oh, I have lots I want to say. But I'm not sure how much of it, if any, is going to make sense."

"Don't worry about that – it's my job to try and help you understand what happened in the past, and maybe see if we can put it in another light."

"I've got a sneaky suspicion you're going to regret saying that."

"Try me." Her warm grin reappeared.

"All right," I said. "Let's start with my boyfriend's death."

Doctor None-of-Your-Business nodded. "I think that's a good place for us to begin, yes. And let me just say, I'm very sorry for your loss."

"Oh no," I said. "It's okay – it wasn't his first."

††

I don't know how to describe what it's like to open up my inbox and see the literally thousands of emails and comments I'm now receiving daily – some of them people reaching out to me, telling me how moved they are by our story, while just as many are sending out vindictive, bitter diatribes, saying they hope I shut up and die sooner rather than later so as to spare them the pain of having to read just one more self-involved entry. And there it is, Internet logic at its finest: because something exists, apparently everyone *must* read it no matter how much it pains them to do so, like some centrist asshole who can't not demand you debate their bullshit ideas on meritocracies in a public forum. You'd think for some people free will really was an illusion. The sense of unearned entitlement is astounding.

It's not all so polarizing, though. I've gotten hundreds of responses from set workers – makeup artists, set decorators, even directors and assistant directors – who remember D_____, for whom he wasn't as invisible as he might have assumed. Or hoped. Many of them have been unexpectedly captivated by what I've written; a few have even gone that extra mile to peer behind the curtain, to comb through the material of our story and try to piece together a visual history of our affair. Some have contacted me privately, asking me to clarify if the couple on screen in this scene or that, at this or that time on the clock, is us – asking why the stories I've told don't always line up with what they see across the many films referenced in my previous entries.

Then there are the duelling late-night television hosts in a bidding war to see who gets exclusive rights to the public, on-air reveal of the jilted, angry, potentially murderous ex-lover behind the world's most prolific living corpse.

Then there's Ezra's vow to *The Hollywood Reporter* that, when the time is right, she intends to come after me with the full force of the legal system behind her. Because saving face is all that matters to her now. I didn't think it possible, but she looks even more ghastly in print than in person. Greed's a helluva drug, I guess. That shit fucks with your very soul.

Then there's the quiet investigation going on into the veracity of my claims – into the potentially hundreds of women killed and flayed for my "amusement," their bodies never found, their deaths never reported.

Then there's D_____. The "villain" of this piece. The world is rapidly contracting around him and still he says nothing. Which is about all I expect at this point.

One last thing I learned from therapy: to know when it's time to move on. I don't want D_____ back. I never have – this blog was never about that. I already knew at the start of all this that there was no chance of us ever being together again, but revisiting our final night as a couple – not to mention the weeks of recovery that followed – has helped make everything crystal clear.

When I began this blog back in November I was furious with him. I'd convinced myself he'd taken something from me – time that I no longer had. But, plainly, anger is exhausting to maintain, and in this instance it accomplishes nothing. I write now because I need to know, when all is said and done and my body has diminished beyond all hope for recovery, that I existed.

31. The Dead Came Knocking

Posted: 05/24/2014

Unnamed Female Love Interest, early thirties (*The Dead Came Knocking*). Temporarily "survived" by her ex-boyfriend, Unnamed Undead Male, mid-forties. Our heroine was a kind person, always willing to open her heart and her door – foolishly, some might say – to a soul in need of salvation. In the first days of the zombie apocalypse, Unnamed Female Love Interest fought hard for her survival, maintaining an upper-level apartment stronghold in which the living were able to find shelter and a temporary reprieve from the evil that hunted them through the streets of Los Angeles.

The Post–Zombie Apocalypse Historical Society acknowledges her sacrifice. God be with the splintered remains of humanity.

††

Bonita Paraiso (*Dead in the Desert*). Together, Bonita and her partner, Claud, were two of the most feared and successful bank robbers this side of the Rio Grande. They stole indiscriminately and looked stylish as fuck all while doing it until their semi-retirement some time ago. When Claud was gunned down during a drug deal gone wrong, Bonita, to make ends meet, to maintain the lifestyle to which she had become accustomed, got back in the game.

It didn't go so well.

††

Wife of Guard 528491 (*Zero Chance, Zero Escape*). Wandered the desolate planet searching for compassionate life.

Found none.

Died alone.

32. All That Viscera Come to the Surface

Posted: 05/30/2014

Stories are beginning to emerge from the outside world. *The Hollywood Reporter* posted an interview on Wednesday with Quinn Margolis, star of such masterpieces as *Sharkopolypse 2: The Second Wave* and the spy thriller/romance *Incognito*. These days, however, she's more widely recognized as Sleeve Zero – otherwise known as the real Malorie Marcello from *The Scorpion and the Frog*.

"No, I don't know who's writing the blog," she said in her interview with *The Hollywood Reporter*. "Shouldn't you be asking the *Los Angeles Times*? The sicko worked there, didn't she? Do they even have an obits writer? I thought that was just something people submitted on their own ..." The interview notes that when contacted, the *Los Angeles Times* editor-in-chief refused to comment on the matter – more than likely under the advisement of their lawyers. "Yeah, I think I remember the guy who played Charlie, but it didn't happen like that – I don't think he and I ever said two words to one another that weren't in the script."

"I've been reading the blog since January," said Felicia Webb, who silently dressed your wounds in *A War to Remember*, to a reporter from the *Huffington Post*. "I don't get it, really, why someone would go to such great lengths to lie about something like this – especially when the truth is so easily unearthed. I can't help but think what a sad and lonely person they must be. I hope there really is a Doctor None-of-Your-Business, and I hope she's able to help this person, I really do."

"I don't know if I agree with all that. Actually, I think it's kind of beautiful." That was Valerie Bedson, your dancing partner from *The Buddy Holly Incident*, in an interview with Celeste Shields yesterday on *Good Morning America*.

"You don't worry this mysterious blogger might be dangerous?" Celeste asked.

Valerie smiled sweetly, lips pressed together. Her eyes showed just a hint of sadness in the way they turned down slightly at the edges. "I don't," she said. "Whatever this person's going through has got to be hard. It's like ... one giant love letter written to the idea of a man but not the man himself."

"So you don't find all that viscera unsettling?"

"I really don't. It isn't real, Celeste. None of it. It's just ... Tragic is what it is."

††

I guess if I'm surprised about anything it's that it's taken this long for things to begin to unravel. And not just for me – I've noticed the resurrection clock on www.risefromthegrave.net has stalled, too. Either their news sources have dried up or you've pulled out of your upcoming contracts for the first time in twenty-one years of doing this type of work.

Or you've been sacked.

Before now I'd not given much thought to the worth, or lack thereof, of a death scene artist with a very public, almost impossible to ignore persona. All this attention being suddenly paid to you has undoubtedly lifted your career from the dregs of celebrity society to C-, maybe even B-list status – welcome now, should you accept their invitations, to the finest couches of daytime television shows and restaurant chain openings. There exists still a gulf between an artist of your calibre and the always eye-catching A-listers, but it is certainly not as wide a gap as it once was, back when you were able to recede like a chameleon into the wallpaper of any party. Without meaning to, I've turned you into a sideshow attraction. For this I am truly sorry. I gave up my identity when we were together, and now I worry that I've taken yours away, as well – what little there was to take, that is. I thought it was what I wanted, for both of us to share in this notoriety, and I think maybe in the beginning it was, but ... Things are different now, and I see the details of our time together more clearly than I once had.

Naomi Weston, film critic for the *San Francisco Chronicle*, wrote a column in yesterday's paper citing this blog as the "single most vicious attack on a celebrity's character in recent memory." In her own words:

> The sporadic entries on the blog *Die First, Ask Questions Later* are nothing more than one jealous individual's indictment of a person, a professional actor, whom they don't know and have likely never met. The assumptions and accusations made therein constitute an open threat to one man's safety, and a breach of the social contract between celebrity and rampant, unchecked fandom. This "fanfiction," as it is, represents the delusional ramblings of a disturbed mind that has, unfortunately, lost all sight of reality. Are we, as readers, to take this love affair as true on any level? We already know the stories of random women being sliced open and zipped up again as full-body catsuits to be an absurd lie, as are this blogger's many increasingly ridiculous acting claims. What, then, of their supposed romantic connection? What of the cancer slowly eating away at the writer's brain? Can anything that's been written be trusted?

> The answer is no, of course not. Because these are not the words of a human but of a broken shell of a person, a transient desperately searching to be made whole again – scrambling through the dark for someone as cold and broken as they happen to be – or seeking someone to whose greatness they only aspire.

The way she slipped *that* word into the middle of her denunciation – *transient* – like it was dirty, coated in a layer of sweat and after-sex. Like she was calling me a whore; a nobody dressed in pigtails and a pinafore dress one moment, and a suit jacket, skirt and tall brunette sleeve the next.

Like I was weak. Like I was nothing.

But I'm stronger than anyone has ever given me credit for. I see it now where I didn't before. Louise, she could never decide how she felt about me, pushing me to go and build a life with one hand while using the other to try and keep me close, to tell me what I was doing wrong. To her I would always be lost, little M______, standing in the mirror, trying on everyone else's face to see what fit best. She helped me, yes, in the beginning, but I wonder now, the times she helped make adjustments to the fit of each face or when she pointed out a suitable skin, if she wasn't so much a partner as I was a project.

Aud ... When I look back on things I think Aud saw me for who I really was. She watched, and she worried, yes, but she never made me feel like I was incompetent, no matter my decisions. "You might be a lost cause," she said to me one night, "but you're my lost cause, ya?"

This isn't for them, though. It isn't for Doctor None-of-Your-Business, either, or for Naomi Weston. It isn't even for the actresses I saw you flirt with so dishonestly from my place behind the camera, or from somewhere just off set, where I watched, reciting your scenes as if I were there, with you, and not forced to pretend I didn't know you until we were alone again, away from curious eyes.

Valerie Bedson was right. As much as I don't want to admit it, I must: This is for you. I'm writing this, at least in part, for you.

33. The Buddy Holly Incident

Posted: 06/03/2014

Eleanor – just Eleanor (*The Buddy Holly Incident*). Eleanor strolled into town one day with a suitcase full of dreams and two nickels to her name. Daughter of Someone Else and Wish I Knew, Eleanor was a bright girl who always had a song in her step. She left home at age seventeen and made her way to the coast, following the never-lasting promise of champagne and made-to-order stardom. While she patiently awaited her big break, she waited tables at Gus's Malt Shoppe, where her all-too-light-on-her-toes attitude made her so impossible to resist.

††

Quiet French Woman (*A War to Remember*). Alone in her cabin in the woods, this unscripted heroine was kind to all and turned none away. One day she dressed a fallen soldier's wounds, only to have him die in her arms – but not before an indescribable love developed between them, like two sparks bonding in silence. Moments later, she died from a broken heart.

34. Natural Born Disasters

Posted: 06/13/2014

It's a strange dichotomy, to feel at once utterly exposed yet totally invisible. I'm like a rat you can't catch, scurrying just out of reach, beneath the trained eyes of all observers. Though my sleeves have been taken from me I still know perfectly well how to hide in plain sight – I've had, after all, a lifetime of practice. I am curious, though, with all Ezra's said to *The Hollywood Reporter*, and in her telephone interview last week with *Access Hollywood*, as to why she's kept my identity under wraps, referring to me only as "the individual in question," who she's been keeping an eye on, because of course the situation is under control and there's nothing to fear, nothing with which to be overly concerned. I wonder though, were I a fly on her wall, if I'd see that it was in fact D_____ who was at least somewhat responsible for her reticence. What did he say to keep her from spilling every jelly bean in the jar? Why? Is it he who's afraid of the ultimate truth getting out or is it her?

I want to tell you about the email I received this morning while eating a day-old bagel I'd picked up half-price from a bakery across the street from the hotel lobby in which I'd spent the night – undisclosed location number nine on my Victim Relocation spreadsheet. It reads:

Dear Anonymous M,

In very little time, your tender, unfortunate life has touched millions. The story you tell of forbidden passion, even as your health wanes, is akin to the great tragic loves of our generation and of generations past. We at Hayfield and James Publishing would like to extend to you the opportunity to gift your story to an even wider audience than you've already reached.

Of course, we would be more than happy, in addition to a sizable advance, to assist in whatever medical costs there may be to get you healthy again.

Please contact our New York offices at your earliest convenience and we will discuss how best to proceed.

Yours,
Christopher Hayfield
Publisher, Hayfield and James

Can you believe it? A book deal with a for really real Big Apple publisher! Because this will benefit my family and I for years to – Oh, right. Well, fuck me.

I suppose I shouldn't be shocked to have received a proposal like this, though I'll admit I'm surprised it took them this long to figure out how best to market this embarrassment of dysfunctions to the public, who are always salivating for new examples of schadenfreude. But to compare this sordid serial to the great love stories of times past is missing the point entirely. Great love stories are Romeo and Juliet (minus the death and familial warfare), Jack and Rose and their big fucking boat, Batman and Robin ... Our history is not, in hindsight, so romantic. We were Mickey and Mallory with guns turned on one another instead of poor pre-rehab Robert Downey Jr. – it was death by mutual attraction and ritualistic self-denial.

It feels redundant to even contemplate selling this story in another format. It's already out there, in the open – it exists, and is available for consumption by anyone with a certain degree of voyeurism in their blood. What good would it do to publish this mess in hard-cover? I guess then the film rights could be optioned – Hollywood could turn lives in film into lives in film *on* film. It'd be an exercise in diminishing returns, like standing between two funhouse mirrors and staring at one's infinitely multiplied self, getting smaller and smaller with each receding reflection.

That's not, however, to say there isn't a market for it. As early as the 1920s the public has foamed at the mouth over famous relationships like the poor survivors of the apocalypse left fighting one another over the world's dwindling supply of canned goods and Twinkies. At first it was only celebrities who garnered such obsession – poor Mary Pickford and Douglas Fairbanks unwittingly paving the road for all who would follow – but it soon became clear that fame was only a part of the equation, and that what people really wanted to see, what they sat in the corners of coffee shops and restaurants and movie theatres listening to, pretending to be oblivious to, was any relationship unfortunate enough to be drawn into a spotlight. They love us, D_____ and I, because we're the covered, dismembered bodies on the side of the road in the immediate aftermath of a highway collision. Because they can't see beneath the clean white shrouds of our sleeves, his and mine, our ragged flesh and shattered bones – because our onlookers don't yet know enough to look away.

"Is that how you see yourself?" asked Doctor None-of-Your-Business near the end of our first session together, once I'd finished telling her about D____, about how we met and how I'd started to see myself – as more of a victim than I really was. I was naive, telling her how I'd been robbed of a future that I know now never existed, that was only ever a dream. "As a body left abandoned by the one you love?"

"I'm not sure how else to phrase it. I was forgotten in less time than it took to spit on the sidewalk." I grew angry, reliving our final moments together for the first time since it all went down – since D_____ left me. "It's like he hollowed me out. I was never really in control, I just thought I was."

"Because you thought it had been you crafting your fiction. But it wasn't."

"What do you mean?"

"You just said you feel as if you've been hollowed out. All those lives you say you created, you weren't really the one building them – you only think you were. But it was D_____ who set the tone every time. You merely followed his example. You feel hollow, M______, because when all the cards are placed on the table you weren't actually his lover. You were, and still are, so long as his actions continue to guide your journey, a puppet."

And then there she was: Aud, back in my brain, cursing me out, telling me to *"live right here, right now, in this motherfucking moment. That's what matters. It's all that matters."* At the time I thought she was right. And I guess to some extent she was – I lived my lives, with D_____, in a way that I needed to at the time. The problem was I never actually let go of thoughts of the future, of what might have been or could possibly be. Futures weren't something that ever interested him, however. And that power dynamic, that gulf between us – me wanting more even if I refused to voice it – allowed him to take control of ... of us. Of the shape of us.

And unfortunately, horribly, *infuriatingly*, Doctor None-of-Your-Business was right. Because there are no bodies, are there? Not really. There are no flayed corpses or stolen identities or pilfered futures littering the back alleys of our tryst – that much of our farce has already been revealed. There are only dreams and ideas that I'd written into the pages of large black binders once shelved at the back of my closet, details of lives – of *possibilities* – learned, memorized, having left nothing to chance. Scripts, all of them. Our "what might have been." They've since been removed, torn to pieces, shredded in a moment of unrestrained fury as you invaded my home, my hollow, puppet, futureless life, searching for, but not ever finding, the origins of us.

35. The Scorpion and the Frog

Posted: 06/15/2014

Malorie Marcello (*The Scorpion and the Frog*).

Malorie fucked the wrong guy.

She watched him die.

They took turns.

36. The Army at the Galaxy Drive-In

Posted: 06/28/2014

For just over a week now I've been staying with a friend of Aud's who reached out to me via direct message on my blog. "Audrey was a dear friend," she said in a private email following our initial correspondence. "We'd worked together at a couple of clubs. She had her demons, but she was a good person and it's clear she really loved you. She'd want to know that you were safe. My home is yours, should you need a place to rest." The timing was impeccable; while my commitment to finish our story remains strong, my strength has been fading for some time now. For the first two days after I arrived on Aud's friend's doorstep – ("Call me Gwen," she said, inviting me inside. "It's not my real name, but ..." "Anonymity," I replied, to which she nodded, smiled and shut the door behind me.) – I slept on a futon in her spare room, a painter's studio. It was filled with half-finished canvases and several plastic bins of squeezed and mangled oil paint tubes, and along the wall, hanging over the window looking out into Gwen's backyard, was a white bedsheet speckled and splattered with a rainbow assortment of hues. Gwen was kind to me – it was more than I deserved. She made me three meals a day and I ate what I could. She even tried to convince me to go to the hospital. "You're so frail," she said as I picked at a chicken salad sandwich she'd prepared for me on our third afternoon together. "A hard wind might break you in two."

"I can't," I said. "They'll send me back home."

"What's wrong with that?"

"There's nothing for me there."

"But ... what is there for you here? Why stay?"

"There's still a lot I don't know," I replied.

Gwen sighed. "I've gone back and read everything, you know. All your entries. It sounds to me like you've already gotten all the answers you're going to get." She tapped a painted nail against the Formica table, the sound an annoying click. "You ... you're not what I expected."

"No one ever is." I finished the sandwich and a glass of orange juice, and started coughing, hacking violently into the back of my hand. "Anyway, it's not good enough yet," I said once the spell had subsided. "I need to know how this ends."

"You know, you're a lot like she was," Gwen said. "Audrey could be so stubborn sometimes. I loved her like she was my sister, but she also didn't know when enough was enough." She took the empty plate and glass away, put them in the kitchen sink to be washed later. "How it all ends," she said, returning from the kitchen, "is up to you. Not him."

"I know that."

"You say you do, but are you being honest with yourself? Or are you just trying to shut me up?"

"No, I know it's up to me. I'll know when I've said enough. It's just ..."

"What?"

I shook my head. "I feel like so far it's just been a bunch of noise. Like I've been wasting my time yelling at a wall that doesn't want to – that isn't going to talk back."

"You told your therapist you didn't care about getting an answer from him – you just wanted to be seen for who you really were." She paused. "He doesn't complete you, you know. He never did."

"Yeah ... Well, I guess when it comes down to it I'm better at lying to myself than I am to everyone else."

"That, and avoiding things."

"I haven't been –"

"All this time, everything you've written, and still you've not said who you really are. You've refrained from putting yourself on the very stage you've created. That's avoidance ..."

"M______."

"Fine then, M______," she said, using my real name. "You're still not clear of all this. And you won't be until you see for yourself just how much things have changed since you started your blog."

"I don't see how that's going to happen," I said. "Not without stepping out into the open and dealing with whatever's waiting for me – good, bad or ugly."

Gwen turned around and grabbed a set of car keys from a ladybug-shaped hook on the wall over the kitchen counter. She dropped them into my open hand. "It's Saturday night," she said. "Take my car and drive out to the Galaxy."

"I've already been there," I said.

"Not recently. You've not seen it like it is now. If you want to see for yourself just how much you've changed things, you need to go back out there."

"What am I looking for?"

"Trust me. You won't be able to miss it."

I took Gwen up on her offer and that night drove out to the Galaxy Drive-In. And do you know what I saw, D_____? Your greatest wish come true – though, I'm sure, not quite like you anticipated. The Galaxy has been resurrected with new life and purpose. The noisy, bustling parking lot was full of hundreds of people, most crammed three or four to a vehicle, with coolers full of beer and soda and green garbage bags of homemade popcorn on the seats between them. There were conversations happening, families and friends gathering, jumping between vehicles and groups like how I imagined it was back in the heyday of the drive-in, when this was *the* place to go on a Friday or Saturday night. When it was more of a party than any standard theatre today. The screen at the far end of the lot remained torn and badly stained in places, but nobody really seemed to care. At the rear of the drive-in, a replacement projector had been installed in the Galaxy's old projection booth – a gift from the owner of a local independent cinema. It was running reel after reel of film – your films, to be exact. The entire scene had a carnivalesque vibe to it as people stood on the tops of their vehicles, or lounged on their backs on the hoods of cars. A small platform had been erected just below the screen, where audience members pantomimed your deaths one after the other. The entire thing was like a morbid fucking re-enactment of *The Rocky Horror Picture Show*, complete with bad homemade costumes and overzealous makeup. They'd made games of your many death scenes – taking shots whenever you died in the arms of another person, or when you'd been given actual lines to deliver. A pair of star-crossed whatevers, who'd probably never met before this night, collapsed into each other's arms, silhouetted by the very same scene playing out on the screen above,. and recited their love for one another before the poison took effect. And when you drove off that cliff with a trunk full of money in *31 Banks*, the entire collective chorused; "Aww, shit!" in perfect synchronicity with your witless onscreen persona.

It was electric. The space was like a carnival that stunk of popcorn, beer and gasoline instead of popcorn, beer and elephant shit – a nominal difference, but a difference all the same. It was like I was there with you all over again, but also not. I joined in when I knew what lines were coming and stayed silent when all I wanted to do was marvel at the amazing sight of so many people gathered for one purpose and one purpose only: to worship you. If Gwen had told me beforehand what to expect, I don't think I would've had the strength, or the courage, to come. I'd have thought that seeing all your deaths again would have been too much for me to bear, but I was completely swept up in the moment. I was your invisible chronicler lost amongst a veritable sea of adoring fans, all of whom had no idea who I was or what I looked like. Who wouldn't have believed me had I jumped onstage and revealed myself for who I am. I looked for you then, wondering if you, too, had somehow heard about this phenomenon. I pictured you in a full trench coat and aviator shades, with a teamless baseball cap pulled down over your face, hiding as much of you as possible and totally not at all looking like a sexual predator out in full view of the world, just stalking silently between parked cars and the people sitting out in the middle of the lot in folding lawn chairs, completely wrapped up in the ridiculous joy of it all.

††

I don't know how much longer I'll be on the move like this. Gwen's been good to me, but I know I can't hide in her home for much longer. It wouldn't be right.

That night, after leaving the Galaxy, I took her car and drove past my old apartment. I parked just down the street, where I could see both the darkened square of my bedroom window and Ezra's vomit-green Mini Cooper S parked on the other side of the road just outside my building. I didn't know how long she'd been there, or if this was a nightly thing for her. I knew she was waiting for me – to call the cops to deport my ass or to send a pair of rent-a-goons after me to bust up my kneecaps I didn't know, and I wasn't too keen on finding out. I was there with just one final job to do, and then I'd be gone. God willing, she'd never see me again. Because the feeling was fucking mutual.

I parked around back, beneath the fire escape, and clambered up to my floor. I went in through the fire exit at the back of the hall – in all the years I'd lived there my landlord had never bothered to repair the fire alarm. For once I was grateful for his negligence. There were no attackers waiting for me outside my front door, no signs of recent entry. I quietly slipped inside.

My apartment was still a mess, my bed and the floor were covered with the remains of the lives I'd pieced together, ripped into confetti and littered indiscriminately. I closed the door behind me and the small resulting gust of wind sent several personality traits and pieces of dialogue fluttering up into the air before they slowly drifted back down again. Tiptoeing over to the window, being sure to keep my face in the darkness, I could see Ezra's bright-pink press-on talons through the windshield of her car, *tap-tap-tapping* on the rim of a coffee tumbler – probably emblazoned with her own damn name, written in glitter and gold – as she waited eagerly for some sign that I had foolishly returned. It's still a marvel to me that she is after all this time refusing to concede defeat. You're more popular than ever, D_____, and I'm sure Ezra is receiving her fair share of the residuals. But this isn't about money, and I'm beginning to think it never really was. She's angry because I pulled you out of the shadows and finally, belatedly, introduced you to the rest of the world. Because, in doing so, I've taken away some of her control over you. But most of all, because you're no longer the secret she needed you to be to remain your one and only. It won't be long now, I imagine, before you get a better offer for representation, and a better cut than anything Bargain Basement Barbie has ever given you.

While Ezra sat with her eyes glued on my apartment, I crouched down and reached under my bed, retrieving a small hatbox I'd hidden up against the wall, behind a spare wool blanket. Inside the hatbox was something special, something I wasn't willing to simply give up. You – or *whoever* had broken in – had missed it your first time through, in your haste to destroy all traces of our time together. I can only imagine how frustrating that must have been, knowing how we began, what we'd written together, our very first draft, but not being able to get your hands on it – not being able to wipe clean from existence our first moments as us.

Were I to hand the hatbox's contents over to you now, though, it wouldn't matter. You will never be able to erase what's happened. Go see for yourself, every Saturday night at the Galaxy Drive-In.

You've been exposed.

You've been seen.

You have a small army at your disposal.

37. Rewriting the Past

Posted: 07/10/2014

COLD OPEN ON BLACK, THE SOUND OF TIRES SCREECHING TO A HALT. THE BRIEF ENSUING SILENCE IS BROKEN BY MUFFLED SCREAMS AND THE DULL THUD OF A FIST PUNCHING THE INSIDE OF A CAR'S TRUNK.

M_____ (V.O.)

You died the day we met.

CUT TO:

EXT: ABANDONED SHIPPING YARD -- NIGHT

CHARLIE ELLINGTON -- AKA "CHARLIE THE CHIN" -- (45-year-old White male) is pulled forcefully from the trunk of a LATE-MODEL BUICK CENTURY and thrown onto the rain-soaked ground. He lands hard on his hands and knees, WINCES. He looks up at his assailant, a tall, outhouse-wide brick of a human named MICKEY O' (late-40s White male).

M_____ (V.O.)

I remember it frame for frame.

(Beat)

I watched from afar as she flirted with you at craft services, as she smiled shyly with seeds in her teeth and you coolly responded by passing her a napkin and a bottle of water but saying nothing in return. She accepted, gratefully, but you weren't listening to her -- you were looking at me, your eyes on mine, and you grinned, seductively, like you knew what I was thinking and were telling me to wait, that you'd come see me when you were finished.

CHARLIE raises his hands up to his face. They're shaking, wet, covered in dirt from where he'd landed on the ground.

CHARLIE

I didn't do it, Mick! I ain't no stoolie, goddamnit! I swear on my grandmother's grave.

M_____ (V.O.)

It didn't matter that it was all lies -- coming from you, it was still beautiful. That was your gift, you know -- like you could steal any scene, so too could you turn even the rankest half-written shit into absolute poetry.

CHARLIE starts to weep openly. He drops his face into his filthy hands.

MICKEY steps in front of CHARLIE. He calmly slips a BLACK LEATHER GLOVE over each hand before reaching around to his back and pulling a HANDGUN from his waistband.

From around the corner of a nearby WAREHOUSE, MALORIE MARCELLO (32-year-old White female) watches as MICKEY screws a SUPPRESSOR to the end of his HANDGUN and presses it against the right side of CHARLIE'S head.

M_____ (V.O.)

My stomach clenched when Mickey put that gun up to your head. I kept myself steady, watching as you emptied yourself of all resolve. Because you were done. Because you were supposed to die. It is scripted and thus it is so.

MICKEY shakes his head. He moves the HANDGUN down, points it instead at CHARLIE'S knee. He FIRES. CHARLIE SCREAMS and falls over on one side, starts writhing in place. Without saying anything, MICKEY walks around to the other side of CHARLIE and points the HANDGUN at CHARLIE'S left arm. He FIRES again. CHARLIE'S SCREAMS INTENSIFY as he flops around on the ground in pain.

M_____ (V.O.)

The crew around me watched gleefully as Mickey tortured you, prolonging your inevitable death. This was a moment they'd all been waiting for -- a key moment in the script where the tables were turned, where Malorie would see the price of crossing her mob boss father in the body of the man she loved. And all I wanted to do was run out from behind the camera, rush the set and tackle Mickey, giving you time -- not much but enough -- to run away.

(Beat)

If I could have, I would have stricken a hard line right through the next page of the script, cut it down, given you a chance to breathe again.

MICKEY steps back, moving in front of CHARLIE, and crouches down to face him. He holds the HANDGUN carelessly between his knees.

MICKEY

C'mon, Chin, take the righteous path here. Admit what you did. Accountability -- ever'thing's about accountability.

CHARLIE musters his remaining strength and lifts up his head. He stares menacingly at MICKEY. Says nothing.

MICKEY stands back up and once more points the HANDGUN at the right side of CHARLIE'S head. He

FIRES a final shot and CHARLIE'S body falls limp. BLOOD pools from his mouth.

Out of sight of MICKEY, MALORIE clamps both hands over her mouth and retreats back around the far side of the WAREHOUSE.

M_____ (V.O.)

And then it happened and I watched, helpless to do anything, as blood flowed out of you like red paint staining your white button-up, caulking the cracks in the pavement with straight lines and ninety-degree turns.

(Beat)

I'd watched your life -- your light -- extinguished in less time than it took to shake someone's hand. It wasn't some stretched out life-before-your-eyes thing you hear people talking about when they drum up the event, making it into something big, into something other than shit. You didn't beg, break or even begin to crack. You took it like the man you were, the man I knew right there and then I was destined to fall in love with.

(Beat)

It was over before it had even begun, and all I could think about was what it felt like last night, when you kissed me -- not as was written in a scene we never actually shared, but in the darkness outside the studio, thinking maybe it'd make a new person out of me. And I wondered then when you'd kiss me next, and if, when that time came, I'd be able to step in and save you before you had to go and die all over again.

38. Letting Go

Posted: 07/11/2014

I stayed with Gwen another couple of days. I was silent that night when I came back from the Galaxy. Right away, when I stepped inside her home, she saw the hatbox under my arm and asked what was inside. I didn't answer, and she nervously asked about what I'd seen at the Galaxy. "I told you," she said elatedly once I'd finished describing what had transpired, the incredible scene I'd witnessed at the drive-in. "You've had more of an impact than you thought. Your story matters to people – *you* matter. You've changed a lot of lives."

Though at first I fought the urge to admit it, Gwen was right. She was also right in one other area: it's time I got clear of all this. There's nothing more I can do – there's nothing more *to* do. Before that night I'd been writing this blog in a bubble. It was about D_____ and me, and about putting all our lies together one after another in a police lineup, where I could see clearly every character he'd played and point them out and say, "That right there, that's the man I fell in love with." And he's the same motherfucker who broke my heart first and my jaw second. Now my bubble has burst and I'm seeing a lot of things more sharply than I have in a long while. It's D_____ who I've succeeded in making transparent, while I remain trapped in the shadows, waiting for my moment, a second-string player with whom he shared only pieces of who he really was. And in everything I've done and tried to do with my life, this blog – *our* story, not mine or any other one I've written, or any of the ones we wrote together, once collected in binders and now strewn across my bed in a rage, and in a hatbox you neglected to find – is the only story anyone wants to hear. The shittiness of the situation is not lost on me.

"I understand," Gwen said when I told her I needed to leave, but not why. "Do you know where you'll go?"

"No," I said, stuffing my laptop into my backpack again and dropping the hatbox into a large shopping bag she'd given me filled with several sandwiches and bottles of water. "Not yet. I need to figure out a few things ... The story still needs an ending."

"Forget the story," she said. "It's time to let it go. Just ... let it all go, M______." She pulled from her pocket a small roll of bills – twenties and a few fifties – tied with an elastic hair band and handed them to me. "A gift," she said, "from me and Aud. For the bus."

"The bus where?"

"Home."

††

My location has changed. I'm in room 1201, at the Howard Johnson just off Manchester, about ten minutes from LAX. There's no sense in hiding where I am anymore – by the time you or Ezra arrives, I'll probably already be dead and gone. The money Gwen gave me would have gotten me home, but as I was standing in the bus depot ready to buy my ticket, I felt my heart swelling uncomfortably in my chest, my pulse racing at the thought of crossing the border again – of seeing Louise for the first time in so long. There was so much between us ... so much I wanted to say but didn't know if I could. I'd run away from that place and made my way here. Going back ... and like this ... I didn't have enough to book a room for more than a few nights but that didn't matter – I figured that was all I had left anyway.

When I look in the mirror now I no longer see myself or anything I once pretended to be – with D_____ or on my own, as a teenager, standing in front of the mirror in the bathroom in my parents' house, trying on the faces of all the neighbourhood children one after the other. What's there now, staring back at me, is sick, a poisonous agent made flesh, with spaghetti string arms and legs and xylophone ribs jutting harshly out from beneath weathered cheesecloth skin. When I exhale my entire body trembles and I feel my fragile legs quivering like they're about to give away. To think I once did this to myself, wilfully, consciously. I'd seen myself a certain way then – not as the person I was but as the person I wanted to be, an image I wanted to attain but couldn't. I tried to become that. I've spent my life trying to be *that*, whatever that is, this impossible to pin down ideal. That's how it is, though. All things, fiction or otherwise, bring with them the baggage of history. My history is one of impermanence. Of not knowing who I wanted to be and letting someone else choose for me. I don't want this, though, not anymore – not my body or any other, and certainly not this tiresome, one-sided conversation.

From the bottom of Gwen's shopping bag I removed the hatbox I'd taken from my apartment and opened it for the first time in more than two years. Folded neatly inside was the loose-leaf skin of Malorie Marcello – a dozen or so hastily typed eight-and-a-half by eleven pages, Courier font. I took out the black-and-white simulacrum I'd created and tried to sheathe myself in it as I once had, back when we first met, but the pages weren't enough anymore – they no longer covered my body as they once did. When I looked down at my hands and saw only my skin – the remnants of Malorie having collected at my feet in a scattered pile of ideas – it appeared weathered and worn out, looking dry and pale and altogether lifeless, and I knew then that it was over.

39. Rethinking the Future

Posted: 07/16/2014

I love learning new things. Even as I near the end, I still feel as if this world has so much to teach me. Four days ago, for example, I learned what *family* really means.

A visitor showed up at my hotel room the day after my last post, arriving early in the morning. I got scared when I heard knocking on my door – I'd been half-expecting the building to come down around me at any moment, but that didn't make it any less terrifying upon hearing a fist just outside my room. I knew it had to be Ezra on the other side – everything inside of me was telling me to run, to somehow get out of there before she called hotel security to open the door and drag my pale, barely ninety-pound ass to the lobby where we'd wait for the nice men with the guns and handcuffs to carry me out the front door and put me on a one-way plane to the other side of the Canadian border.

Then, a muffled voice from the other side of the door: "M______? Open up. It's me. It's Louise."

And I was somehow more frightened than I'd been only a moment earlier.

"M______, I just want to talk."

There was tenderness in her voice. I recognized it immediately – I'd last heard her sound like that when she was saying goodbye to me in the early morning hours so many years ago, pressing a wad of cash into my hand and urging me to run away from home and go make something of myself.

She knocked again. "M______, please, I know you're in there."

There was nothing I could do. No place I could run to and hide. And I knew my sister well enough to know that I would lose in a war of attrition. I took a deep breath and opened the door.

And sure enough she was there, looking older than I remembered but still as beautiful as she'd always been. She was dressed head to toe in navy blue sweats and was carrying a small red overnight bag over her right shoulder. Her hair had thick streaks of grey in it that weren't there the last time I saw her, and heavy crow's feet that had been enduringly stitched beneath her narrow, sleepless eyes. Upon seeing me in person for the first time in more than a decade she flinched, tightened her grip on the strap of her overnight bag. I heard a sharp intake of air like a punctured bike tire.

"Oh my god ..." She started to cry.

And then I started to cry.

She dropped her bag and pulled me forcefully into her arms, damn near pushing all the air out of my lungs in the process.

"I never thought I'd see you again," she said.

"I ... H-how did you find me?" I asked.

She pulled back and wiped her eyes and nose with the back of her hand. Her face was red and tear-streaked. "You posted your location, you dummy."

"You ... were reading?"

She nodded. "Since January. I didn't say anything before now because ... I didn't know what to say. There was just too much." She looked down at my body, at the hotel bathrobe that nearly doubled my girth. "I had no idea you were so ... Oh god, M______, I'm so sorry."

She pulled me into her arms again, gently, carefully, and said she was foolish and stubborn to have let things fall apart as they had. She begged me to forgive her and I did the very same, and we held each other for what seemed like hours and –

And that's all you're going to get – you and everyone else reading this. Because Louise is real. She came to me that day, and she showed me that she loved me – that no matter how much shit there is between the sheets, family is family. I'd long believed that not all blood is family, and that not all family is blood. I still do – people like Aud and Gwen were there for me in ways few others have ever been – but Louise had, in that moment, done more than I ever anticipated. I had selfishly left her to bury our mother alone because I'd fallen in love with an idea I didn't know how to quit; she'd come back to me because she wasn't willing to let that happen again.

What Louise and I said to one another that afternoon will never be written, here or anywhere else. Those moments were ours and ours alone. They die with me.

That was four days ago. Today, while slowly scraping away at a plate of scrambled eggs and toast in Louise and Mark's condo overlooking Vancouver's English Bay, I learned a second new thing: I learned the true definition of irony.

What did I see when I returned to www.risefromthegrave.net? They'd taken down D_____'s Jesus clock. As a matter of fact, the site's entire home page had been overhauled, changed from its gothic-black predecessor to a soft milky white, like a shower curtain or a freshly laundered sheet had been draped across. It was a full minimalist redesign with only a single all-text news story posted right smack in the centre of the page:

> David Ericcson, star of nearly 800 feature films and television series, will be starring next as Dr. Irving Merchant on the upcoming NBC drama *Merchant of Mercy*.

> "We're delighted to offer David this once-in-a-lifetime star-making turn," says executive producer and showrunner Seth Wildman. "David has proven himself more than capable as an actor, and we think it's about time he got his moment to shine."
>
> When asked whether or not Ericcson's recent acquisition as a first-time lead on a weekly drama was, in fact, a response to the unprecedented growth of his cult celebrity status as the unwitting star of the scandalous *Die First, Ask Questions Later* blog, Wildman responded by saying, "Whatever David's past with that individual is or was doesn't matter to us or to the viewing public. We see him only for the powerhouse of raw talent he really is. We're proud to have him join our team."

Star. Of nearly eight hundred features and television programs. It's official: the dead are now more memorable than the living. Though I suppose that's always been the case – we do better remembering those who've changed the world only after the fact, when they're gone and we're left to ponder their existence. I feel like I should congratulate David, but I'm simply unable to wrap my mind around this: him, on a weekly series, to be watched and recognized by millions. Tens of millions. As far as commitment is concerned, this one-eighty is, to say the least, impressive. A lesser person might try to take credit for his sudden excess of wealth and attention, and I might have done just that were I not so sure he was taking this job to once more try to prove he's something he's not and never will be. Inside, I imagine, he is scared to death. For that, I take no pleasure.

These entries are getting harder and harder to write. The space between, though, is filled with memories unwilling to slow to my body's pace. While lying in bed this morning, I remembered a brief conversation we had while he was between takes on *The Buddy Holly Incident*. I'd just brought him his coffee – oh, the glamorous life of a set runner with delusions of ambition and talent. He told me, in a rare moment of transparency, arms folded on top of the camera between us with his face mere inches from mine, how he never really wanted to get his "big break." "They're for people who want to live in the world," he said when I asked how long he wanted to keep going like he was. "Those people ... they want the world to change them. I don't want that. I don't want to be just another product of my environment."

"You want your environment to be a product of you," I said.

And he nodded, and smirked knowingly, and went back to work. And you know what, fuck that sly, I'm-so-brilliant grin. That line's from *The Departed*, you unoriginal asshole.

And now he's going into it – the big scary world – to be changed by an audience now watching his every move, where before they'd been oblivious to his existence. Well then, maybe congratulations are in order.

Meanwhile, here I am, dressed all in white and ready to death-do-us-part and he's gone ahead and decided to live without me.

Okay, so maybe I do take some pleasure in it.

It's complicated, though. There's pleasure, knowing that maybe I've forced his hand at change, but there's hope, too. There's always been hope. That maybe this will be the right fit for him. That maybe he'll start to see things, and me, differently.

That maybe I made an impact. That maybe I was someone special after all.

There's hope, too, in death. There has to be, otherwise we'd lose ourselves to despair. Hope that we're lucky enough to leave something more than a footprint so easily covered in our absence. That we learn and have learned from all the little deaths we die each and every day. The thousands of times we die each year, only to get up and die all over again because that's what you're fucking supposed to do. That's what we're all supposed to do. Every single knife in the gut, every shred of pain and humiliation and anxiety and envy that shears us to the bone, they're how we know we've been a part of something. The world, places in it, people's lives. *Our* lives. They're real, those myriad deaths. Maybe they don't feel it when we look back at them from the end of the final reel, but they happened. They happened all the same. They were lessons, all.

Your deaths were not. Are not. They're immaterial. They're nothing, because you haven't actually owned them. They've been extravagant, sure, sometimes; sometimes they've been subtle and unexpected. Always they have been art. But art is nothing if an artist chooses not to live in this world. To be of this world – which you now are. Ostensibly. Hopefully.

Your deaths, like us, like you, David, and like me, were and have always been a fiction.

I want to know: Are you out there now? Are you receiving me? Are you hidden among my audience like I imagined you were that night I went to the Galaxy and saw, with my own eyes, just how loved you are? I hope so. I do. I really do. And for what it's worth, I hope you enjoy your life, David. Your new life. I hope it is everything for you that I could never be. That death never was.

I hope you know how special you are.

I hope

I hope

40. Remembering What Was

Posted: 08/20/2014

**Louise's note: I found this next to M_____'s bed on their last day. They'd been working on it here and there for a few days, when they weren't … I'm not sure if it's finished, but here it is anyway:*

††

Morgan Alexander Farris (1981–2014) died in the early morning hours of August 15th from complications resulting from a malignant brain tumour.

They wanted more than anything for you to see them before they died, to just see them for who they truly were, when the lights were on, but you never did – you never came. You never took the time to look at what was there, beneath the surface, how similar the two of you were and yet how completely, utterly not.

They are survived by their older sister, Louise Elizabeth Farris.

Thank you for the flowers.

Acknowledgements

A novel doesn't happen in a vacuum.

Behind every word of this book is an entire community of friends, family and loved ones who've had my back from minute one, and who, for some strange and unknown reason, continue to stand by me through all my anxieties, obsessions, sarcasm and garbage sleeping habits that no intelligent human would endorse.

The team at Wolsak & Wynn/Buckrider Books: to Paul Vermeersch and Noelle Allen I owe a debt that I will never be able to repay. They saw something in this story that they thought worth championing, and I am beyond grateful for their confidence, in both this book and me. And thanks as well to Ashley Hisson, for her amazing edits and for helping to shepherd this book across the finish line.

The Death Scene Artist would not be what it is without the incomparable Jen Sookfong Lee. Her edits, kindness and support throughout this process helped transform this book from something I was happy with to a thing of which I am immeasurably proud. Jen, you are amazing, and I am so fortunate to have gotten the chance to know you and work with you.

Of Michel Vrana, I am in awe. With a single image he managed to perfectly capture the look and feel of my story. Michel, your cover is thoughtful, beautifully rendered and above all a work of art, and I am privileged to have it.

And of course no one would be reading this were it not for Kelvin Kong, who stuck by this book, and me, through two years of rejections – the sting from each felt as much by him, and sometimes more. I'm lucky to have him as my agent, but even luckier to have him as a friend.

Speaking of friends (and family, and friends who are family), there are many more yet to embarrass, all of who played a part in bringing this story to life.

My thanks to Sandra Kasturi, who edited a much earlier, skeletal version of this novel, and helped me to see all the ways in which it was simply not ready for prime time.

And thanks, as well, to Michael Matheson for being a constant, caring, encouraging ear for this book and all things writing (and so many other things as well); to Julia Horel, for her unceasing friendship, at-all-hours pep talks and for celebrating this book with me every step of the way; and to beta readers Tan Light, Raivenne McKinnon, Monica Miller, Angel Vats and Heather Toler – for your friendship, your honesty and your willingness to point out all the ways my work could improve, including but not limited to pulling my own head out of my ass.

To my family: my parents, Darrel and Ross, who've provided me with an incredible amount of love and support for my creative endeavours, without fail, my entire life (even when it was not financially prudent to do so); and my siblings, Elizabeth and Blair, who are almost entirely to blame for my sense of humour and various pop culture obsessions.

To my partner in crime, Jaime Patterson, who entered my life shortly after I first started work on this story and has been by my side the entire way, I give my thanks and my love. I could not have made it this far without you.

And to Carol Diana Patterson, my cheerleader. You are loved, and you are missed.

ANDREW WILMOT is a writer, editor and painter living in Toronto, ON. He holds a BFA in Visual Arts (with a minor in Film and Video Studies) and a master's degree in Publishing, both from Simon Fraser University. He has won awards for screenwriting and short fiction, with credits including Found Press, *The Singularity*, *Glittership*, *Turn to Ash*, *Augur* and the anthologies *Those Who Makes Us: Canadian Creature, Myth, and Monster Stories* and *Restless: An Anthology of Ghost Stories, Dark Fantasy, and Creepy Tales*. As an editor, he's worked with Drawn & Quarterly, ChiZine Publications, Broken River Books, ARP Books, Playwrights Canada Press, Freehand Books, Wolsak & Wynn and NeWest Press, and is a freelance academic editor specializing in matters of body dysmorphia and eating disorders. Books he's worked on have taken home multiple awards from the Sunburst Awards, the Eisner Awards and, most recently, the Shirley Jackson Awards. He is also co-publisher and co-EIC of the online magazine *Anathema: Spec from the Margins*. *The Death Scene Artist* is his first novel. Find him online at: andrewwilmot.ca, anathemaspec.tumblr.com and on Twitter, hating everything about Twitter, @AGAWilmot.